CW01497702

BILLIONAIRE ROMANCE
COMPLETE SERIES

MONTGOMERY BILLIONAIRE SERIES BOOKS 1-3

MICHELLE LOVE

CONTENTS

Made in "The United States" by:

Michelle Love

© Copyright 2020 – Michelle Love

ISBN: 978-1-64808-229-0

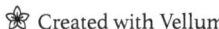 Created with Vellum

ABOUT THE AUTHOR

Mrs. Love writes about smart, sexy women and the hot alpha billionaires who love them. She has found her own happily ever after with her dream husband and adorable 6 and 2 year old kids.

Currently, Michelle is hard at work on the next book in the series, and trying to stay off the Internet.

"Thank you for supporting an indie author. Anything you can do, whether it be writing a review, or even simply telling a fellow reader that you enjoyed this. Thanks

facebook.com/HotAndSteamyRomance
instagram.com/michellesromance

BLURB

Sloan Whitlock is a busy woman. Entering her final semester of grad school, she's completely focused on her work, but when a misunderstanding threatens her life, everything changes.

Lucas Montgomery was one of the wealthiest and most successful men in the city, and he's not used to hearing the word no. When he catches sight of Sloan at Club 9, he knows he has to have her. She was a vision of innocence, and he was desperate to have a taste.

Someone is out to ruin Lucas and Sloan becomes a target merely because the person behind it all can see that Lucas is looking at Sloan with more than a little interest.

Kidnappings, attempted murders, and more come between to two as they grasp at having some sort of a relationship. The odds are against them. Then the unimaginable occurs and love is found beyond the lust they share.

Can this couple find the happiness that is evading them? Can their stubborn personalities work together to work to save not only their lives but their relationship as well? Or will the person behind the plot to ruin the handsome billionaire get what they want and ruin them all?

BOOK ONE: WHEN HE DESIRES

DESIRE, DANGER, LUST

Sloan Whitlock is a busy woman. Entering her final semester of grad school, she's completely focused on her work, but when a misunderstanding threatens her life, everything changes.

Lucas Montgomery was one of the wealthiest and most successful men in the city, and he's not used to hearing the word no. When he catches sight of Sloan at Club 9, he knows he has to have her. She was a vision of innocence, and he's desperate to have a taste.

She meant nothing to him until someone decided that Lucas would pay dearly for her safety. Now she has to rely on him to protect her, and attraction between them heats up. Common sense tells her to keep him at arm's length, but her body burns for him.

Can he keep her safe and convince her to change her mind?

CHAPTER ONE

Sloan

The music pumped through the speakers, and I swayed lightly on the balls of my feet. I wasn't much of a dancer, but it didn't look like anyone else in the club could dance either. The floor was so packed that bodies rubbed up against each other as they jumped and gyrated. Shoved into a corner, I gripped a bottle of beer in one hand and kept a tight grip on my phone in the other.

Sweaty and more than a little drunk, my roommate Randi danced her way to me and snagged my beer. Taking a long sip, she frowned at me. "Sloan, that phone better be out because you're collecting phone numbers from hot guys," she yelled at me.

"I'm just checking it," I shouted back over the base of the music. "The dress is too damn short, and I'm afraid it's going to fall out!" Because the dress she forced me to wear didn't have any pockets, I had my card, car key, and phone strapped in a small pouch against my thigh. It was a little uncomfortable, but I knew that I'd lose a purse if I tried to bring it.

"Girl, that dress looks sexy as hell!" She handed me back my beer and turned to smile at the man standing next to me. Randi was an exotic beauty. In a city of fake tans, her own Latin blessed skin was always dark and smooth. Her streaked dark hair fell to the middle of the back, and she had those perfectly pouty lips. Everywhere we went, she drew the attention of most of the male population.

And, if I were being honest, quite a few females as well.

I, on the other hand, was easily overlooked. No matter how hard I tried, my Irish skin refused to tan. My long auburn hair curled on a good day but usually stayed in a tangled frizzy mess. To tame it, I usually kept it pulled back either in a bun or tied at the nape of my neck. I tried to cut it once, but it was a year-long disaster. I wasn't the kind of woman to spend any significant amount of time in front of the mirror primping and preening, so my hair was a mess that could not be tamed.

I wasn't a complete disaster. I do have nice green eyes, but I was already forced to wear reading glasses. As a student, my nose was usually stuck in a book, and the glasses felt like a permanent fixture on my face.

These days, looks were not all that important to me. I was one semester short of graduating with my Master's in Childhood Education. I was a busy girl.

Tonight was Randi's birthday, and she literally threatened me with hell and high water if I didn't go out with her. Disgusted with most of my own clothes, she squeezed my curves into a short and slinky green halter dress. I felt completely exposed.

"You haven't danced with a single guy since we got here," she accused me. "We're supposed to be having fun!"

"You're supposed to be having fun," I corrected her. "And from what I can tell, you're having a ton of fun. Let me get you a drink, and you can find your next victim."

"You're impossible," she growled, but she didn't stop me as I leaned over the bar and waved down the bartender. One good thing about my outfit was that I didn't have to wait for my drinks. My tits were practically spilling out of my top, and the bartender couldn't stop looking at them.

"A tequila shot for my friend. No training wheel," I ordered. He stared at my cleavage the whole time he poured.

"You should give him your number," Randi muttered in my ear.

I just shook my head. While I was pretending to enjoy myself, the truth was that I was scrolling through the latest email from Professor Elliot. My advisor had pretty much torn my thesis idea to shreds. Of course, at the end he had written excellent start.

What the hell did that even mean? I couldn't help but obsess.

Randi downed her tequila shot and scanned the crowd. I knew she was looking for her next dance partner, but suddenly, she reached over and grabbed my arm. "Sloan," she shouted in my ear. "That guy is staring at you."

"He's probably staring at you," I said absently as I held my empty beer bottle up. The bartender popped the cap off another one and handed it to me.

Her nails dug almost painfully into my skin. "Believe me, I wish he was staring at me. He's got to be the sexiest guy in here."

Curious, I turned around to follow her line of sight. Above us, on the second floor balcony, the man leaned over the bannister. Randi wasn't lying. He looked like sin personified. Dark hair swept low over piercing blue eyes and curled at the nape of his neck. His stubble didn't do anything to hide his strong square jaw, and it was clear that he was tall and built.

Chills raced down my spine. He did seem to be staring at me. I'd indulged in some loaded fries earlier. Maybe I had parsley stuck in my teeth. Self-consciously, I turned and ran my tongue over them before I tilted back my beer.

"Go talk to him," Randi urged me.

"Hell, no," I muttered. It was too quiet for her to hear, but I'm sure she knew exactly what I had said. Randi had been my best friend and roommate for two years. She knew my weaknesses and limitations. I didn't talk to men. Lately, I'd been hiding behind the fact that I was so busy with school, but she knew that I was still hurt from my last relationship.

My one and only boyfriend, Victor Willis, had spent two years keeping me down before I realized he was cheating on me. That was six months ago, and I hadn't even tried to hook up with anyone since.

"Suit yourself. I'm going to go dance." Randi gave me a disgusted look before heading back to the dance floor. Two of her friends had made it to the edge, and she sandwiched herself between them and gave everyone quite a show.

I envied Randi's confidence. She could use her body like a weapon, but she was also brilliant. As a student of childhood psychology, she was often the driving force behind my teaching theories, but while I had to spend almost every minute working, she could go on a weekend bender and still ace her Monday test.

Once again left to my own device, I returned my attention back to my phone. I typed a quick reminder to myself when someone rammed into me.

Gasping, I stumbled back and dumped my beer all over myself.

"Damn it," I swore. Looking up, I tried to pinpoint the culprit, but there were too many people near me, and no one was paying any attention.

"At least it's not my dress," I grumbled as I leaned over the bar to grab some cocktail napkins. "Can I get some club soda?" I asked loudly.

To the dismay of some of the other patrons waiting, the bartender moved quickly to fulfill my request. Holding my phone between my teeth, I tried to maneuver through the crowd until I burst onto the patio. "I had a little accident," I explained to the bouncer who stared at me like I'd lost my mind. Deeply breathing in the fresh air, I dipped the napkin in the club soda and tried to dab at my dress. I didn't know what I expected it to do. It wasn't just a little spot. The beer had spread from the straps all the way to my midriff and was slowly soaking through my skin.

My cleavage was sticky, and I reeked. Disgusted, I tossed the napkins and left the glass on the table. I kept several changes of clothes in the trunk of my car, and there was a tank-top and jeans in there that would get me through the rest of the night. Snagging my keys from the small pouch, I opened the gate of the patio and slipped out.

I'd just made it to the car when a dark van came to a squealing halt in front of me. My heart stopped when the door slid open.

Son of a bitch. I was about to be kidnapped not more than twenty feet from a crowded club.

The first masked man jumped out, and I could feel his eyes raking over me. "Damn. Lucas Montgomery is going to pay handsomely for your safe return."

Who the hell was Lucas Montgomery?

"I don't have any cash," I said as I tried to keep my voice calm. "And I don't know any Lucas Montgomery."

The masked man snickered. "From the way he was looking at you, I bet he knows you quite intimately. No one looks at a woman like that unless he's already licked every inch of her skin."

I shuddered and fisted the key in my palm so the metal edge stuck out between my fingers. If he thought I was going to meekly get in the van, he had another thing coming.

The two of them tried to grab me, and I moved. I wasn't a

Kung-Fu master, but I'd learned a few things from the kick-boxing classes Randi had dragged me to, and I'd taken more than a few defense classes. I swung my key around to dig it into one guy's eye and lashed out with my foot. It connected solidly with the guy's nuts, and he screamed and hit his knees.

Dodging my key, the man wrenched me around and slammed me against the car. Fear coursed through me, and I kicked out wildly again. I didn't hit anything, but it was enough to make him move. He pulled me roughly to the ground and wildly looked up. "Come on," he yelled as he grabbed the abductor still moaning on the pavement.

I guess I had caused too much of a scene. By the time I'd pushed myself off the loose gravel, they'd jumped back in the van and were gone.

CHAPTER TWO

Lucas

She was captivating. I couldn't help but stare as I caught sight of her. After a two long and boring hours of an investment meeting, I was ready for a drink, but watching her was better than a shot of whiskey.

It was obvious that she was completely out of place. When she wasn't staring at her phone, she was constantly tugging on her green dress. First she'd pull it up in an effort to hide her ample cleavage, and then she'd tug it down to cover more of her creamy thighs. I was already lost in a fantasy of what I would do to her if we were alone.

What would I touch first? Her tits were just begging to be held, but I also desperately needed to fill my palms with her ass. I wanted to pull out the clip that held her curls and yank her hair back until I could press my lips to the column of her neck. I wanted to yank her dress up and discover what kind of treasures she was hiding underneath. Would she be hiding a black lacy thong? Pearly white panties with bows? Maybe she was naked underneath, and I could sink my fingers inside her.

I was the kind of man who didn't have to look far for a beautiful body to warm my bed, but there was a distinctive downfall to having so many women to choose from. It took more work to excite me, but one look at her, and my cock was already rising to the occasion.

Fuck. The blonde that I'd tied to my bed last night didn't even have this effect on me, and she'd been very talented with her mouth.

The mystery woman's friend said something in her ear, and she looked right at me. When her gaze met mine, I saw her eyes widen as she took me in. Her lips parted in surprise, and she suddenly whirled around. Amused, I straightened and started walking to the stairwell. I craved her. I'd pull her on the dance floor and hold her against me. It was so crowded tonight that I could easily flick my fingers over her clit until she came in the middle of all the other horny dancers.

Then I'd take her home and fuck her until she screamed.

Just as I reached the top of the stairwell, the bouncer grabbed my arm. "Mr. Montgomery? There's a phone call for you."

Of course there was. With a sigh, I headed back to the VIP room where the young waitress handed me the phone. She was a cute little brunette with a smile that said she knew she was attractive. If there was one good thing I could say about the club, it was that the owner knew how to staff it.

The glass separated me from the rest of the clubbers, but the floor still vibrated with the base, and I could still faintly hear the music. At the back, a private bar was fully stocked with only the finest liquors.

"Montgomery," I growled into the receiver.

"You're not picking up your cell," Steinburg growled. Howard Steinburg was my Vice President of operations, and he'd been stressing over the investment meeting. While it was my money to do as I pleased, investing in Club 9 would have been a public move. He was concerned about how it would reflect on my character and my company.

Steinburg worried too much, but that's why I kept him on.

"It's a club," I growled. "I can barely hear my own thoughts, let alone my damn phone. What is so important that it couldn't wait until morning?"

"How did the meeting go?" Steinburg was a good twenty years older than my own thirty-two. He always liked to say that he was too old for pleasantries.

I turned around to watch the dancers below. "The numbers are good. The club has done well for the past six months, but I have a feeling it's just a trend. In a few more months, it'll be old news, and it'll die just like the other ninety percent of the clubs in the city. I told the owner that I would think about it, but I don't think it's going to make me any money."

Steinburg sighed in relief, and I couldn't help but smile. I wasn't exactly the golden child of the media, but the press wasn't knocking down my door in search of scandal. The city had come to know me as a perpetual bachelor and playboy, but I didn't break hearts or cause drama. Still, Steinburg made sure that my PR agents stayed on top of things. He'd been pissed when I told him that the manager of Club 9 had invited me to an investment meeting.

I was careful with where I invested my money, and I fielded offers on a weekly basis. It was rare for me to actually attend these meetings, but Club 9 was all the rage these days, and while I wouldn't be investing, I was happy that I took the meeting.

As Steinburg blabbered on about how I had made the right decision, my mind wandered to the delicious treat downstairs. "Steinburg," I said abruptly. "This is all stuff that you can tell me on Monday during normal business hours. Go to bed. Men your age went to sleep hours ago."

"One day, if you're lucky, you'll get to my age and you won't think those jokes are so funny," he snapped. Without bothering to say goodbye, he hung up the phone. I chuckled as I put the phone back on the receiver and headed out of the room. The small second floor lounge served as overflow, but because it didn't have a bar or dance floor, it was mostly for people trying to take phone calls or hide from club creepers. The glass windows separated it from the VIP room, but heavy curtains obstructed the view.

Leaning over the bannister again, I scanned the main floor for the woman, but she was nowhere to be found. Irritated that I had lost her, I headed back to the VIP lounge to exit out the back private entrance of the club.

My faithful driver, Danny O'Brien, had been with me for almost five years now. Although he'd moved from Ireland more than a decade ago, he still held fast to his Irish accent. He told me it was because it drove women crazy, but I had a feeling that Danny felt a little lost sometimes. Like everybody else, he needed something to remind him of home. A man in his late forties, he'd been married to the same woman since he was eighteen years old.

His wife was terrifying.

"Going home alone, Mr. Montgomery?" Danny was one of the few members of the staff who spoke freely to me. Although he was always polite, he rarely filtered his words.

I was not a fan of the backseat, so unless I was making a public appearance somewhere or riding with another passenger, I almost always sat up in the front with Danny. I was much more comfortable in the driver's seat, but I always had Danny drive me when I knew that I would be drinking.

"It wasn't a successful night," I muttered before ducking into the car. The dark steel colored Bentley Continental GTC was my favorite car in my collection.

"Unsuccessful because you're going home alone or because the investment didn't work out like you wanted?" Danny teased as he started the car. The engine purred rather than roared, and I settled back in the leather seat.

"Both," I said wryly. "I had my eyes on a beautiful wallflower, but Steinburg had to call and pull me away. I lost her."

"Wallflower? That'll be different," Danny commented with a sly grin.

As we pulled out to the main street, several police cars flew past us with their lights flashing. "Just because you have to go home to the same woman every night doesn't give you the right to judge my own love life," I muttered as I watched the police cars. They were pulling into the club parking lot. What had happened?

"I get to go home to the same woman ever night," Danny corrected. "And it's not really a love life unless you actually cultivate more than a one-night stand."

"Turn around." I wanted to see what all the commotion was all about.

Danny obeyed without comment and within minutes, he parked close to the police cars. "What happened here?"

"That's what I intend to find out. Stay here and keep the engine running. I won't be long." Exiting the car, I walked slowly to the closest officer as I took in the scene. A small crowd had gathered, and the police were still taping off a small section of the parking lot. In the middle of everything, one officer was draping a blanket across the shoulders of a woman.

My wallflower. As I took in the tangled mess of curls and green dress, I felt an invisible fist punch me in the stomach. "Excuse me. What's going on?"

"No questions," the officer said gruffly as he tried to wave me away.

"I'm Lucas Montgomery," I said quietly. "I was just inside a few minutes ago." It was rare for me to drop my name like that. Normally people knew who I was, and if they didn't know, I didn't care to tell them.

The officer's eyes widened. "Did you just say Montgomery? Hold on just a minute. Don't move." He ran over to someone else and, after a few seconds of conversation, waved me in. I ducked under the tape.

"Mr. Montgomery, I'm Detective Allen. Are you familiar with a Sloan Whitlow?"

I noted that the detective had flipped open a notepad. "I'm not," I said slowly.

The detective pointed to the woman behind him. Paramedics were still checking Sloan out. "That's her. You have no idea who she is?"

"I saw her in the club, but I've never seen her before tonight, and I didn't know her name. If you're asking if I witnessed anything, the answer is no. I'm just here out of curiosity."

"Curiosity, huh? Are you the Montgomery from Montgomery Industries?" Allen asked. His eyes gazed at me shrewdly.

I knew when I was being interrogated. Peeved, I shook my head. "I'm not answering any more questions until you tell me what happened. Otherwise, you can talk to my lawyer."

"I apologize for the third degree, Mr. Montgomery. You're not a suspect, but it took me by surprise when you showed up at the crime scene. Ms. Whitlow contends that while she was at her car, two men tried to abduct her. They said that Lucas Montgomery would pay for her return. She says that she has no idea who you are or what you do. She must have fought like hell to get away."

"Is she okay?"

"A few scrapes from the pavement. Nothing severe. She's a very lucky woman. Do you think she knows who you are?"

Immediately, I clenched my teeth. "She's probably telling the truth. I did see her at the club, and I may have exhibited some signs of interest. Anyone watching me may have misconstrued that."

"Did you walk to her? Dance with her? Buy her a drink?"

"No," I said softly. "She was by the bar on the first floor, and I was on the second floor by the stairs leading up to the VIP room. I just watched her."

"It must have been some look that you gave her," the detective said softly. "Leave a number where we can contact you if we need to. There are cameras in the parking lot, but apparently the men were masked. We may have some further questions for you."

I rattled off my cellphone number as I stared at Sloan. As if she knew that I was watching her, she turned her head and locked eyes with me. Her mouth parted in surprise, and I knew that she recognized me from the bar.

Rather than go talk to her, I thanked the officer and headed back to my car. I wasn't quite ready to speak to her yet, but I did need to get more information about her. If she had been harmed because of me, I wanted to keep an eye on her. And if she were running some kind of game, I wanted to know.

There was just something about her that I wasn't quite ready to let go of yet.

CHAPTER THREE

Sloan

The blue lights flashed around me, and I wrapped the blanket tighter around my body. The officer took my statement, and the paramedic kept urging me to go to the hospital. The attack kept flashing in my mind.

"Damn. Lucas Montgomery is going to pay handsomely for your safe return."

It couldn't have lasted more than a few minutes, but it felt like an eternity. My skin still burned from where I'd scraped it on the pavement, and loose gravel still bit into the palms of my hand.

The paramedic interrupted my thoughts, and I blinked. "I'm sorry. I didn't hear you."

"That's okay. There isn't a whole lot more we can do, but if you feel any type of unusual pain, you need to get to a hospital. Do you understand?"

I nodded my head and tried to smile at him. As he packed his bag, I felt the heat of someone staring at me. Turning my head, I felt shock jolt through me. The gorgeous stranger from the club was speaking to the detective and watching me. Dropping the blanket from my shoulders, I took a couple steps towards him, but he had already turned and disappeared into the crowd.

"Excuse me, Detective? Who was that man that you were just speaking with?"

Detective Allen gazed at me steadily. "Why? Do you recognize him?"

Immediately, I flushed. After everything that had happened, I felt strange telling the detective that I needed the name of the man that made me wet with just one look. "He was watching me at the club," I said lamely.

"I didn't realize a man could cause so much trouble with just one look," the detective muttered. "That's Lucas Montgomery."

"What?" I gasped. "I don't understand. Is he someone important?"

The detective snorted. "He owns Montgomery Industries. He's one of the richest men in the city."

"I don't pay much attention to business," I said softly. "What did he say to you? Does he know who attacked me?"

"He wanted to know what happened and if you were okay. Says he doesn't know you and doesn't know why someone would think that he'd pay ransom for you."

Rubbing my arms, I nodded. An angry shout drew my attention past him to the crowd where Randi was screaming at an officer.

"She's my roommate," I said as I rushed over. "It's okay."

"Sloan!" Randi wailed. "What the hell happened? These assholes wouldn't let me talk to you. Are you okay? Do I need to kill someone?"

"It's her birthday. She's a little drunk," I apologized to the officer as I grabbed her arm. "Randi, maybe don't offer to kill a police officer. I'm okay. I'll explain everything later."

"Ms. Whitlow, do you want an officer to escort you home?"

A shiver of fear slid down my spine. Was there any chance that the men knew where I lived? "It might be nice if someone followed us." I swallowed hard and squeezed Randi's arm.

"Officer Jackson will follow you," the detective said with a nod. "Go home and try to get some sleep. I'll let you know if I have any further questions."

Nodding, I pulled Randi through the small taped off area. Before I could get in the car, she threw her arms around me.

"I was so scared when I saw all the police lights and couldn't find you in the club," she whispered in my ear.

Holding her tightly, my eyes scanned the parking lot for any sign of the would-be kidnappers or for Lucas Montgomery. "Come on," I murmured. "Let's go home."

I desperately needed a shot of tequila and a long hot shower. Anything to help keep the nightmares that would surely haunt me tonight at bay.

By MONDAY, I had pushed Friday night's horrific events to the back of my mind. Determined to focus on school, I'd spent most of the weekend in the library, and now the only thing that split my focus was the image of Lucas Montgomery.

No matter how hard I tried, I couldn't stop thinking of him. He'd looked at me like I was a main course.

I kind of wanted to be his main course.

"Hi, Sloan."

Locking the front door to my apartment behind me, I turned to the sound of the soft spoken voice. Matthew was our next-door neighbor, but we didn't know much about him. He looked to be somewhere in his thirties, and he was attractive in a dark and brooding way, but he rarely said more than just hello and goodbye. I had no idea what he did for a living, and I never saw anyone go in or out of the apartment with him. He kept strange hours, and we never heard a peep from his apartment. No television or music blaring. Trish felt sure that he was a serial killer.

"Hi, Matthew. How was your weekend?"

"Fine." Without offering any more information, he opened his door and left me standing in the open courtyard.

I don't even know why he bothered to say hi at all. Grumbling, I tucked a strand of hair behind my ear and started walking towards my car. Our apartment building stood three stories high and surrounded the courtyard. The company did a good job of maintaining a small garden in the middle, so it was always pretty to look at. The top two levels had railed walk-ways that overlooked everything, but those of us on the first floor had a small patio where we could put out chairs. Because we were so close to the university, most of my neighbors were students, so we were all friendly with each other.

Matthew was an exception.

When I reached my car, I saw a dark car in the overflow parking spot near my apartment. It wouldn't have caught my attention except that it had been there all weekend. Every time I saw it, it looked like there was a person inside.

Like surveillance. Detective Allen had offered me security detail if I felt like I was in danger, but it seemed unlikely that the kidnappers would know where I lived, so I had turned it down. Maybe he was having me followed anyway.

They stayed parked as I pulled out of the complex, so I pushed that out of my mind as well. I had three classes today, and I hoped to squeeze in some time to work on my thesis.

Campus was in full swing by the time I pulled in to one of the student parking lots. Since it was early, most of the students rushed to class with cups of coffee in their hands. I had already had two cups this morning, and while I loved to stop at the campus coffee shop, I probably needed to cool it with the caffeine.

It wasn't until my last class that I realized that I was being followed. When I passed the Business Center building, I could see their reflections in the tinted glass. When I stood in line at the dining hall, I saw them lounging by the entrance. And when I headed back to the library, I just had a feeling that if I turned around, they'd be no more than a few feet behind me.

Turning the corner, I bumped into a hard body. Books and papers spilled on the floor. "Watch where you're going," a younger woman snapped.

"I'm sorry," I muttered. Bending down, I tried to help pick up her things, but I kept looking over my shoulder. "Did you see two guys in suits following me?"

"Paranoid much? Lay off the rooms." She grabbed the book out of my hand and stalked off in a huff.

"Rude," I muttered, but she was right. I did sound paranoid. Maybe I hadn't shaken off the attack like I'd thought. Feeling like a crazy person, I gripped the strap of my bag and quickly climbed the steps to the library. Only people with student or faculty passes were allowed inside, so if anyone was following me, I'd lose them inside.

But the hairs on the back of my neck never went down.

CHAPTER FOUR

Lucas

"Mr. Montgomery, Mr. Hamburg is here to see you." Cecilia poked her head in my door and gave me a friendly smile in an effort to soften the blow.

I grunted my displeasure and wrinkled my nose. "Did he say what he wanted?"

Hamburg was a member of the board, and he was always a thorn in my side. Still, it was unusual for him to stop by for an unscheduled meeting. Cecilia gave me a pained look. "I'm afraid not." She was a pretty woman a few years older than myself. Single, but I'd never been tempted. Not only did she had three kids, but I didn't mix business with pleasure. She'd come to me as a temp, and we'd worked well together, so I had hired her full time.

"I have a conference call in Tokyo in ten minutes, but it shouldn't keep me too long. See if he wants a cup of coffee. If he wants to see a specific department, get Walsh to take him."

Gordon Walsh was my personal assistant. He'd started as an eager intern, and a year later he still hadn't lost his irritating cheerfulness. But he was organized and energetic, so I kept him on as well.

"Yes, sir. Would you like me to bring you a coffee as well?"

"No. That's Walsh's job," I grumbled.

I knew she was about to argue, so I look pointedly at the clock to usher her out. She closed the door quietly behind her, and I pulled my notebook from my briefcase. My production line in Tokyo was still in its early stages, and they had to check in every week with updates. Normally someone else would take the calls, but the last time I had tried to expand to Tokyo, the deal went disastrously South. I didn't need any more black marks against me in Japan.

Despite the stress that my company put on my shoulders, my office was my place of peace. Large and sparsely decorated, it had a wall of glass that overlooked the city below. I despised clutter, so my desk was neat and organized. I had a couch for when I wanted to relax, Bluetooth speakers for when I needed music, and a television for when I needed to watch the news. It connected to my own private bathroom and shower, so when I needed to take a break and go for a run or do some push-ups, I would wash up afterward. The door locked automatically behind me. My retina scan got me in, and several members of the company had key cards that could override the system. Here, I felt in control.

My phone vibrated, distracting me. The text message was quick and simple. I think she's made us.

Damn it. I had four men tailing Sloan Whitlow. They rotated throughout the day, and they were supposed to keep her safe, but they were also supposed to keep their distance. She was never supposed to know that they were there.

Annoyed, I texted them back. Not okay. Keep me updated.

Logically, it was not my fault that someone had tried to

kidnap her, but I couldn't help but feel guilty. It would have been obvious to anyone at the club that I was interested in her.

More than interested. She'd been on the forefront of my mind all weekend, and even now, the image of her haunted me. My inner voice taunted me. Maybe I wanted her to realize that I was having men follow her. Maybe I wanted a reason to talk to her again.

"Konnichiwa, Mr. Montgomery." The video feed popped up on the computer, and the representative bowed to me. "How are you this evening?"

"It's still morning here," I grunted and held up my coffee. "I appreciate you staying up late."

"We are used to it. Progress is good. We have filled almost all the employment slots. We have a mountain of applications."

I paid my employees well, so I expected nothing less. I demanded a lot from the people who worked for me, but I compensated them accordingly. "Good. How is the construction going?"

The man cringed. "I'm afraid it still looks a week behind schedule."

"My contract for the builder only gives a four-week margin of error. If they push it behind anymore, they'll be breeching the contract, and I'll find someone else who can finish the job. And I won't hesitate to do that. I'd rather waste time finding a new builder than work with someone who can't meet my demands," I said harshly.

"Of course. I'll make sure they know that."

"See that you do. Email me their response." The small red light on my phone indicating that my secretary wanted to speak to me started to blink, and I ended the conversation with Japan and pushed it. "Yes?"

"I'm sorry to bother you again, Mr. Montgomery. Mr. Hamburg is insistent that he needs to see you right away."

The damn man was pushy. I sighed and shook my head. "That's fine, Cecilia. I've wrapped up my conference call. Send him in." I pushed the button under my desk that unlocked my door.

The door clicked, and Cecilia swung it open and led Hamburg in. He was a tall, portly man with thinning gray hair and shrewd dark eyes. Of all the board members, he was the least irritating, but he was also the most involved. Most of the members only showed up during meetings, but Hamburg liked to call frequently with new ideas. He'd recently retired from his own company, and I think he missed the action. I usually welcomed his ideas. He had a mind for business.

"Hamburg," I said as I rose from my desk. Grabbing his hand, I shook it firmly and gestured to the empty seat. "What brings you in today?"

He sank into the seat and took a few deep breaths. Years of drinking, smoking, and poor eating were taking a toll on him. "Montgomery. I'm sorry for barging into your office, but there is something that I thought you should see." He reached into his inner jacket pocket and slid a newspaper across the table. The Boston Times. Narrowing my eyes, I unfolded the paper and scanned over the headline.

"Montgomery Industries to buy up prime Boston real estate." I read. "What the fuck is this shit? We just voted on the expansion last month. I haven't even set up an appointment with real estate, and we sure as hell haven't bought any property yet."

"I doubt anyone would have even noticed had I not had some connections in Boston," Hamburg said. "Someone thought they could leak information without it reaching you."

I quickly read through the article. "My public relations department doesn't even take phone calls from the press unless we're unveiling a project or dealing with a public issue. Any reporter calling for more details would have been ignored," I murmured. "Hamburg, that was a closed door meeting, and all the information in this article is correct."

"I know."

His words hung heavily between us. He didn't dare come right out and accuse the members of leaking the information, but we both knew that there were few other explanations. "I'll have security sweep the room for bugs," I said stiffly. "None of this is damaging information, but I don't want to risk any critical information reaching the public before we're ready."

"Bugs. Right," he said with a wry smile. "And if you don't find any?"

"Then we follow normal protocol. You all signed a transparency agreement with the company. If the majority of the board agrees, I'll be able to pull financial records. Let's hope it doesn't come to that."

The older man nodded. He pursed his lips, and I could see the wheels in his head turning. "If I were you, I wouldn't announce the leak to the board just yet. It could cause unneeded duress. There is nothing more dangerous than powerful men who don't trust each other in the same room. If you can't find a reasonable explanation for the leak, you could set up private meetings with each board member and feed them each a different false lead. When the story is leaked, you'll have your man."

I nodded. "Excellent idea. Let's hope it doesn't come to that. I'll have my team do a search each day to make sure that no other information is out there. Is there anything else I can do for you while you're here?"

"You could give me the number for your secretary," he said with a devious smile.

"And have your wife beating down my door? I don't think so." I rose again and shook his hand. "If you're so inclined, my assistant will walk you around. Feel free to talk with anyone that you like."

"Can Cecilia give me the tour?" he pushed.

"Absolutely not," I said with a grin. "Thank you again, Hamburg. And I appreciate your discretion on the matter."

As he nodded his head, I walked around the desk and opened the door. When Hamburg exited, I noticed Torrence leaning over Cecilia's desk. She was deeply enthralled in their conversation, and neither noticed me standing there. I cleared my throat, and he jumped away guiltily.

"Montgomery," he said as he cleared his voice. "I was just coming to see you."

"Really?" I asked with a raised eyebrow. "Or are you here to see my secretary?"

"I just told him that you were in a meeting," Cecilia said hastily. I cocked my head and stared at her. In all the time that I had known her, she had never been nervous around anyone before.

"Where the hell is Walsh?" I growled. "I want him to show Hamburg around."

"I'll page him immediately," she said as she reached for the phone.

"Hamburg, behave yourself while you wait," I said in a low voice. "Torrence, come in."

My security gave Hamburg a suspicious look before walking through the door. "Why would he not behave himself?" Torrence demanded.

"I trust you're not here to question the actions of a board member," I said mildly as I closed the door.

"No. I'm here because the police called. Why didn't you tell me about the incident at the club? You have four of my men tailing some strange girl? They're hired to protect you, and that's hard to do when you leave out pertinent information and keep them from the building," he said sharply.

Torrence was pushing forty. He worked as part of my father's security detail, and he was the only man I'd ever consider to run my own security. We'd been friends for a long time. He was married to the job, and he took personal offense when I did anything to make that job even harder.

"I didn't say anything because the attack wasn't targeted at me," I said calmly. "And I'm protecting the woman because I'm the reason she was harmed in the first place."

"Not targeted at you? Someone wants to hurt you through other people. How is that not targeted at you?" Torrence snapped.

"They don't want me. They want my money. And if you really want to help, you'll look into it so I don't have to worry about it." I sat down and stared at him.

"Lucas, we've been lucky so far. The most I have to deal with is angry activists. In order for me to keep it that way, you need to let me know when something like this happens. I've looked at the police report. There isn't much to go on. The plates on the van were stolen, and the men wore masks, so we can't run them through the facial recognition database."

I blinked. "The police just gave you the report?" I asked suspiciously.

"Sure. We'll go with that. I want to speak to Mrs. Whitlow."

"Ms. Whitlow," I said automatically. He narrowed his eyes and watched me as I hesitated. I could see where Torrence was coming from, but as much as I wanted to see my wallflower again, I wasn't sure it was a good idea. "I wanted her followed at a distance, but I think she's already suspicious. I'll have her brought in tomorrow."

"Good. Next time you withhold information from me, I'll kill you myself."

"I don't see why you're so upset. If I had told you, you wouldn't have had a reason to come up and flirt with my secretary," I said coolly. He narrowed his eyes, and I smirked. "Before you go, I need you to quietly sweep the board conference room for bugs."

He raised an eyebrow, but he didn't ask any questions. I felt almost guilty as I watched the door close. Normally I would brush this kind of situation aside. As cold as it seemed, I was far too busy to deal with every little infraction, but my body burned to see her again.

Was I making things worse for her just so I could insinuate myself into her life?

CHAPTER FIVE

Sloan

It wasn't my imagination. Someone was following me. When I walked out of the courtyard from my apartment, the same dark car was parked in the overflow parking lot. Only this time, two men were standing outside the car.

My heart pounded against my chest as I froze on the sidewalk. I was torn between making a break for my car or turning and heading back into the safety of my apartment. They approached me before I could make a decision, and I reached into my bag to grip my pepper spray.

"Ms. Whitlow?" the tall one asked.

I ripped the can out and aimed it. As I sprayed it, I screamed at the top of my lungs. "Get away from me!"

They both covered their eyes, and I turned to run. Before I could get far, one of them wrapped their arms around her. "Ms. Whitlow, stop! We work for Mr. Montgomery! We're just trying to protect you!"

I struggled against him. "You really expect me to fall for that, you creep!"

"If you give us a minute, we can call him," he grunted. The tall one walked around us and gasped as he wiped his eyes. Pulling out his phone, he held it up to his ear. "Mr. Montgomery? We're having some issues." He turned his back to me and spoke in a low voice.

I stopped struggling, and after a minute, he put the phone up to my ear. "Ms. Whitlow, this is Lucas Montgomery. I assure you that my men don't mean you any harm. I just wanted to have a word with you."

"They've been following me for days," I spat.

"Yes. I was concerned for your safety."

Even though I'd never heard him speak, I somehow knew that it was him. His voice matched him. Quiet and intense. Controlled and authoritative.

Seductive.

Tempting.

"I'm listening," I said quietly.

"You misunderstand. I would like to speak to you at my offices."

"I can't come see you right now. I have class," I said as I took a deep breath. It settled me, and the man finally let me go.

"This class is more important than your safety?" he asked mildly.

I rolled my eyes. "Pretty much. Look, if you have information that I'm in immediate danger, you need to tell me so I can call the police. Otherwise, you're just being a little dramatic. Give me the address, and I'll meet you this afternoon."

He paused, and I bit my lip. Maybe I'd been too harsh. I didn't even know him, but he made me feel extremely uncomfortable, and I was lashing out. "Your last class is at two. My men will drive you to campus and shadow you until then. They'll drive you straight here."

"How the hell do you know my schedule?" I exclaimed, but

he'd already hung up the phone. "Is he always like this?" I asked as I returned the phone.

"Yes," the tall man said grimly.

The day seemed to crawl by, and I couldn't even begin to concentrate on my classes. I don't even think I heard a single word about the lecture on children's literature. I should have just gone to see Lucas in the morning and been late. At least then the day may not have been such a complete waste.

By the time my last class ended, my hands were shaking. I had no idea what to expect from Lucas Montgomery.

The car pulled up to the front of the skyscraper labeled Montgomery Industries and kept it running as I stepped out. No one followed me, and I turned back around. "Are you coming?"

"No. The receptionist at the front desk will you show you to Mr. Montgomery's office."

"Which floor does he own?"

"All of them."

They drove away, and I stood, stunned, on the sidewalk. All of them? I knew he was wealthy, but there had to be close to a hundred floors. How could they all be his?

Nervously, I pulled open the glass door and walked into the bright and open lobby. A young woman smiled at me, but before I could say anything to her, a man stepped in front of me.

"Ms. Whitlow?" he asked sternly.

I blinked. Damn. He looked good. Older than me, but his rugged features were really working for him. "Yes," I said softly.

"I'm Drew Torrence, head of security. I'll take you up to see Montgomery." As he guided me to the back of the lobby, he pulled out a badge and held it up to the elevator. The doors immediately opened. "This is the executive elevator. It's the only one that leads to the top floor."

"That sounds nice," I said lamely. Jesus. Nice? Was this how my conversation with Lucas was going to go as well? "So you're security? Does that mean that you're looking into the men who tried to kidnap me, or do you just protect the offices?"

"I protect Montgomery," he said shortly.

He didn't offer any more information, and I didn't ask. It was clear from his stance that he didn't like me very much, and I didn't have the courage to ask him why. I had a sinking feeling that he could strangle me in the elevator, and no one would blink an eye.

The doors opened, and I quickly rushed out of it. The short hallway had huge windows running from ceiling to floor, and I had a breathtaking view of the city. It almost made me dizzy to realize how high up I was. I didn't have a fear of heights, but I don't think I'd ever been anywhere that had that kind of view.

The door down the hall opened, and a young man came rushing out. He looked determined and almost terrified as he made a beeline for the elevator. I quickly stepped out of the way.

"Please forgive Gordon. He's always full of energy," a woman said from behind a large desk. "I'm Cecilia. Mr. Montgomery will see you now." She smiled warmly at me, but when she saw Torrence behind me, her cheeks reddened slightly, and she looked down.

"Thank you," I murmured. Rather than following me into the office, Torrence leaned against the wall and stared at Cecilia. I had no idea what the story was between them, but the tension was enough to set the damn building on fire.

Opening the door, I couldn't help but gasp. To call it an office was an understatement. The executive suite had three doors that led into other rooms, and a huge leather sofa placed along the wall. A large flat screen television sat over the door, and a well-stocked wet bar ran the entire length of one of the walls.

"Impressed?"

His voice wrapped around me, and I froze. Leaning against one of the door frames, he stared at me. He was dressed in a crisp white shirt that was rolled up to his elbows and dark slacks. It was clear that his outfit probably cost more than I spent in a month. I tugged nervously at my jeans and t-shirt. "It's nice," I said hoarsely. "Mr. Montgomery, I presume?"

"Nice?" he chuckled. "I suppose that will have to do. Please call me Lucas. Can I offer you something to drink?"

Mutely, I shook my head. Drinking around him could be a dangerous thing. "Why am I here?" I blurted out.

He poured himself a drink and gestured to the empty chair. I sat down, and he leaned back in the leather chair behind his desk. I couldn't stop the image that popped inside my head.

Me, kneeling on the desk as he plunged inside me from behind.

Gasping, I wrapped my arms around myself. What the hell was wrong with me?

"Are you okay?" he asked as he stared at me.

"I will be once you tell me what I'm doing here. I appreciate you thinking that you have to protect me, but I don't know you."

"I don't think that will help you," he said as he sat his drink down. "I showed interest in you at the club Friday night, and it was enough for someone to think that we were somehow connected. I would be upset if they tried again."

I couldn't help but shiver. "I don't think someone would get that impression just from you looking at me," I muttered. "It's clearly just a misunderstanding. I'm probably not even in danger anymore."

"You're clearly uncomfortable around me. You're protecting your body and avoiding looking directly at me. Over the phone you were sassy and dominant, but when you're close to me, you're quiet and submissive. Either my office makes you uncomfortable, or I do. I'm inclined to believe the latter. My office is very inviting. Anyone watching you now would see the interest in your eyes. Anyone watching me would know that I was attracted to you. That I wanted to get to know you much more intimately." His voice was low and silky as he tried to make his point.

I trembled under his words. If he could make me wet just from talking to me, I could only imagine what would happen if he touched me. Whatever was between us was both intense and stifling, and it terrified me. When I got scared, I got mean. "You're a complete stranger, and you're telling me that you find me attractive. Any woman would feel uncomfortable," I snapped. "The club is a highly sexualized place. It's designed to be a breeding ground for desire and lust, but when you portray those same qualities in a professional atmosphere, it's uncomfortable."

"Those are all valid points. If it will make you more comfortable, I'll try to avoid portraying my desire and lust," he said dryly. I immediately flushed. He probably thought I was a complete idiot.

"Let's just get back to the reason why I'm here. You think having me followed is an appropriate response, but I thought I was being stalked. You can't just try and protect someone without telling them," I muttered. Lowering my arms, I tried to seem more assertive and comfortable.

"They weren't supposed to be so obvious, but now that you're aware of it, you don't have anything to fear."

My eyes widened. "You're going to keep having me followed? The police are going to find who tried to kidnap me, and it's highly unlikely that they know where I live. You should be more concerned about the people close to you. They're the real targets."

"I am having them watched as well. Sloan, I'm not going to remove your security. You can argue until your last breath, but I don't change my mind easily. Like it or not, we're going to become quite close until the deal is settled."

Outraged, I stood. "You're really not great at listening to people, are you? Before Friday night, I didn't even know your name. Stalking is a crime. If you don't leave me alone, I will call the police."

"Well," he said with a small smile. "You're not uncomfortable now, are you? I'll make you a deal. Allow my men to keep an eye on you for the rest of the week. This Friday, allow me to convince you to accept my protection when I take you out. If you still no longer want it, I'll leave you alone."

My eyes narrowed, and I regarded him suspiciously. "Where would we be going?"

"If I told you, it wouldn't be as much fun, would it? I'll be in touch with you." His words were final, as if the conversation were over.

"Damn it, I haven't agreed to anything!"

"The only time a woman should use profane language is when they're in pain or in the throes of pleasure."

His voice was hard, and my jaw dropped. In one sentence he'd enraged me and turned me on, and I had a feeling the bastard knew it. "Fuck you," I snapped. Turning on my heels, I stormed out of his office.

It wasn't until I was in the elevator that I could breathe easily again. Despite having the last word, I knew that I hadn't won the conversation. He would continue to have me followed.

And I'd be forced to see him again on Friday.

It was hard enough to be near him in the office. How was I going to react in a more private setting?

"You are in way over your head, Sloan," I muttered.

CHAPTER SIX

Lucas

When I called her earlier, I'd requested that she wear the green dress from the club last weekend. She opened the door in jeans and a sparkly tank-top. I couldn't help but smile. She was a mess.

"Is this going to take long? I have an early morning tomorrow," she asked as she grabbed her purse. If I hadn't caught the look in her eye, I would have thought that she was irritated. But her pupils dilated as soon as she caught sight of me.

She liked what she saw.

"You're a college student. You're supposed to enjoy your Friday nights and sleep in all day on Saturday." While her back was to me, I took a moment to drink her in. Despite the casual dress, she looked phenomenal. The long sleeveless shirt didn't quite cover how well her ass filled out those jeans, and for a brief moment, I enjoyed the fantasy of running the palm of my hand over it.

"I'm a graduate student. Friday nights don't exist and Saturdays are for research," she muttered as she straightened.

Turning to face me, she pulled her unruly hair back and pulled it through a band. "We're both in agreement. If I go with you, you'll leave me alone?"

"Is that what you want?"

"A simple yes or no would be fine," she snapped.

"Yes. If, after tonight, you want me to withdraw my protection, I'll honor your wishes. But if you get kidnapped, I won't be paying the ransom."

"Fine. I'd hate to be in your debt anyway." She glared at me and waved her hands to shoo me out of the doorway.

"Why don't you like me?" I asked as I watched her lock the door.

"You nearly got me kidnapped. You're stalking me. You're incredibly inappropriate, and you actually tried to pick out my outfit for tonight. I've had all of one conversation with you. Just because you are rich doesn't mean you get to control my life. Are you going to tell me now where we're going?"

There weren't many people who spoke freely to me. Strangers certainly didn't speak to me that way. Women didn't speak to me that way. "Just dinner."

"Dinner? That's not vague at all." She tucked the keys in her purse and turned to face me. The moon bathed her in light. She looked ethereal. Far too pure for someone like me.

But I wasn't about to let that get in my way. I was certain that by the end of the evening, I'll finally have tasted her. And if things really went well, I might taste more than just her mouth.

Her apartment was quaint and small but well maintained. I put my hand on the small of her back to lead her to the car where Danny waited. Her muscles tightened under my touch, but she didn't turn away. I was tempted to slip her shirt up and touch her bare skin, but I knew that she would push me away.

As instructed, Danny didn't say anything when he opened the door. She thanked him politely and slid into the furthest corner of the luxury car. Amused, I kept the distance that she seemed to need.

She nervously chatted during the short ride into the city. Our destination, Wu tong Shen, was named for the five Chinese deities that represented lust and carnal desire. They were known for their power to possess and ravish beautiful women.

Despite its name and reputation, Wu tong Shen had a reservation list that lasted months. Their food was excellent, and the entertainment enticing. The restaurant catered to all different tastes. The more restrained could enjoy a normal restaurant on the first floor. The more daring could enjoy the erotic entertainment on the second floor, and those that had a standing invitation like myself could book a private third floor.

"Wu tong Shen?" she asked in alarm. "I know the food is good, but I've heard what they do on the second floor."

"We won't be dining on the second floor, my little wallflower."

Her eyes flickered at the nickname, but she didn't comment on it. We walked in, and she glanced suspiciously around the restaurant. It looked very much like an expensive five-star restaurant. White table cloths, flickering candles, silver trays, and a serving staff dressed in formal wear. Sloan was far too underdressed, and she knew it the moment we walked in.

"Mr. Montgomery," the hostess said warmly. "It's always a pleasure to see you."

She was fresh and young, but she wasn't allowed above the first floor. The owners were very strict about the rules, and it's what kept the place running smoothly. When it first opened, the press eagerly came in search of scandal, but they left disappointed. It went above and beyond the legal requirements of a strip club. Tips were encouraged, but the cover fee to get upstairs was more than enough to keep the local ruffians at bay.

We could have taken the stairs to the third floor, but the

hostess walked us to the elevator instead. Sloan dragged her feet, and I pushed her gently. "You said we weren't going to the second floor," she said nervously when the doors closed.

"We're not." I smiled when she bit her lip uncertainly. She was so innocent. I wanted so badly to dirty her just a little.

The door opened up to a hallway. The third floor was sectioned off into four closed rooms. Only four reservations could enjoy the third floor at a time, but they were allowed to stay as long as they wanted. I ushered her down the hall to the last door on the left. When I knocked, the door opened to reveal a small dining area.

Dark leather booths lined the walls, and a small table stood in the middle of it. Like the tables downstairs, it was covered in a white cloth but I had specifically requested the candle be removed.

"You have your own private dining room here?" she asked in confusion as she glanced around.

"Not me specifically. The four rooms can be rented for prescreened individuals for a fee."

"Why do they have to be prescreened?"

"These rooms are private for a reason," I said vaguely. She glanced at the gentleman who had opened the door, and he smiled indulgently and held out his arm. I allowed him to escort her to the table and pull out her chair. She seemed delighted in the experience.

"I have to say, this is not what I expected."

I took my own seat, and the gentleman turned to me. "Who will you be requesting, this evening?"

"Sandra will be fine. Thank you."

He looked surprised but merely nodded and quietly left the room.

"You have your own waitress?" she asked as she opened the menu. "That's awfully fancy."

It was time to chip away at her innocence just a little. "Each of the women and men who work up here are designed to satisfy. Individual satisfaction. If you want your waitress to serve you naked, it's allowed. If you want to eat your meal off her body, it's allowed. And if you want to watch her engage in certain activities during your meal, it's allowed."

Her jaw dropped. "That's illegal," she whispered.

"The one thing you are not allowed to do is fuck the waitresses or ask them to pleasure you. You're welcome to ask them to join you when they get off work, but it's not allowed here in the restaurant. Nothing illegal happens here."

She shifted uncomfortably in her seat. I could tell she was embarrassed to ask, but she finally let curiosity win. "What sort of activities could you request?"

"The staff are very close. If they're so inclined, they can pleasure themselves or each other while you watch."

The blood drained from her face, and her eyes widened. "I guess I knew that kind of thing was popular, but I didn't think there were places designed for it."

"I believe it's required for the staff on the third floor to enjoy being watched. They get off on it," I said quietly.

"How many times have you watched?" She looked almost horrified after asking and quickly shook her head. "Never mind. I don't want to know."

I smiled indulgently. "I am quite fond of the food here, and I like the privacy the third floor provides. I have never requested anything special here, but if you're curious, I'd be happy to change that."

"No," she said quickly. "I don't think I'd like that. Why would you even bring me to a place like this?"

From the way she was gripping her menu, I knew she probably might like it a little too much. Did she get off on watching other people? Or did she like the idea of someone watching her?

"I told you. I like the food and privacy. I'm fond of the filet's here, but if you like seafood, the stuffed flounder is divine."

"We're just here to eat and talk?"

"Does that disappoint you?" I asked her quietly.

"Of course not."

We both knew she was lying.

CHAPTER SEVEN

Sloan

My body ached to be touched. Had he taken me to a normal restaurant, I would have still been turned on by him, but the thought of what might be happening on the r side of the wall nearly pushed me over the edge. Just because it wasn't prostitution didn't mean this wasn't a sex club.

Expensive, but a sex club none-the-less.

Sandra, the waitress he'd requested, did not serve us naked. She wore an incredibly slinky dress, and if she bent over, I knew that we'd get an excellent view of an area that's supposed to remain private. She was attractive, her voice was sultry, and she couldn't keep her eyes off Lucas.

I couldn't even believe how jealous it made me.

Downing the glass of red wine in front of me, I tried to enjoy the food. It really was delicious, but it paled in comparison to the other hunger that grew inside me. I was never the kind of girl who had fantasies about strangers or sex in public, but that wasn't stopping the film of torrid fantasies that continued to play in my mind.

"You're supposed to be convincing me why I need your protection," I reminded him. It was something to distract me.

He swirled his glass of whiskey around and cocked his head. "I watched the video feed from the surveillance cameras. You put up quite a fight, but there was only one thing that worked in your favor. You were in a parking lot of a crowded club. Because you didn't come easily, they were afraid that you'd attracted too much attention to them. You stay late at the campus library. What if they had caught you in the deserted parking lot at midnight? What if they had attacked outside your apartment when everyone was asleep? You defended yourself, but they could have overpowered you."

The thought had occurred to me, but I didn't want to think about it. "That doesn't explain why I need your protection. By now they probably know that we're not in a relationship, and they've moved on. It would be ridiculous to try again."

"Would it?" he asked quietly. "Even if we weren't acquaintances before, we certainly are now. I have no family in the area. I have no close friends that are easily accessible, and I don't date. If they decided to try again, targeting you is the only real choice. They've pushed you into my life, and I can no longer call you a stranger. It would be no small thing for them to request a million dollars for you. That's pocket change to me. I'd shell it out without a second thought."

A million dollars was pocket change to him? I almost asked how much he was worth and decided that I really didn't want to know the answer. "All of that assumes that they'll even try again. They've already failed, and they know that the police are investigating and that I'm being watched."

"But if you decide that you don't want my protection, you won't be watched anymore. My head of security did his research. They weren't there by chance. That same van has been tailing me for days. It's quite possible that they were going to try and take me hostage and demand that my company pay for my return, but you became a much easier target. You still are an easier target. They've put in an awful lot of effort to give up after one failed attempt. The police don't have their names or identities. They choose another vehicle, and they´ll try again."

Shuddering, I pushed my plate away. I had suddenly lost my appetite. As much as I hated to admit it, he had a point. It didn't make sense that they saw me and hatched a kidnapping scheme. Of course they'd planned something. It was too much to be a coincidence.

Sandra came in and cleared our plates. "Will there be anything else that you'd like to enjoy?' she asked seductively. I couldn't help but glare at her. I know I wasn't gorgeous, but I wasn't invisible.

"Sloan?" he asked in a low voice. "Would you care for dessert?"

He probably didn't mean a piece of chocolate cake. Reddening, I shook my head, and he smiled at Sandra. "Some privacy then. Thank you for your services."

Was it my imagination or was she snarling at me with her eyes? I tried to return the look, but she only rolled her eyes and stalked out of the room. "I think she was disappointed," I said dryly. Pushing my chair back, I folded the napkin and placed it on the table.

Lucas stood as well. "Going somewhere?"

"The meal is over," I said, confused. "I figured we were done."

"We're not. I think that the only reason I am where I am now is because I'm a careful man. I'm not willing to take any chances." He moved slowly around the table, and I was torn between the urge to flee and stand my ground. "I have the means to protect you. You should take advantage."

He closed the distance between us. As I leaned against the table, his hands settled on my hips, and I couldn't help but place my hands on his chest. I couldn't explain the pull I felt towards him, but it seemed that I was powerless to stop it. "Is that the only thing I should be taking advantage of?" I asked breathlessly.

Chuckling, he slipped his hands under my top and skimmed the pads of fingers across my skin. His hands were strangely rough, and they awoke every nerve in my body. Desire coiled low in my belly, and I arched my back.

"Do you know what I was thinking when I saw you for the first time at Club 9?" he whispered in my ear. My head rolled to the side, as his fingers caressed my belly. A single finger skimmed under the waistband of my jeans, and I moaned.

Fuck. Anyone who looked up right now would think that I was ready to take him right on the table. Maybe I was.

"I wanted to know what you would sound like when I touched you. I wanted to know where all your sensitive spots were. I wanted to know how you would react to my touch. I wanted to slide my hand under that dress and see just how wet you were."

I tried desperately to find my grip on reality. "You didn't even know who I was." His body was warm and hard beneath my touch. I wanted to be as brave as he was. I wanted to lift his shirt and press my lips to his chest.

"Knowing who you are doesn't change the way my cock reacts to you," he said harshly as he pulled me from the table. I'd barely had time to react before he sat in a chair and pulled me across his lap. As I straddled him, I couldn't help but buck my pussy against him. We were both fully clothed, but I was desperate for any kind of relief.

"Tell me what you like, Sloan. I'll take you anyway you want tonight. I'll fuck you senseless right across this table. No one will bother us." He fisted my hair and yanked my head back so he could graze teeth down my neck.

He hadn't even kissed me, but I already belonged to him. Every bone in my body screamed for his touch, but in the middle of the sexual haze that surrounded us, a single moment of clarity had me arching away from his body. I wasn't some toy for him to amuse himself with.

"And when I no longer need your protection? What happens to me then?"

He frowned, but he didn't stop touching me. Sliding the hem of my shirt up even higher, he grazed his thumb over my bra. My nipples immediately puckered. "What do you mean?" he asked quietly.

"You know damn well what I'm asking. You use your money and charm to seduce women, but how long does it last? One night. One week? Maybe a month if they're lucky?"

"Tell me that you don't want me," he commanded as he dug his fingers into my sides. "Tell me that you're not curious about us?"

"I want you. More than I've ever wanted anyone. So much so that it doesn't even make sense to me, but I'm not going to be just a tally for you." I yanked his hands away and slid off his lap. The more space I put between us, the more I could think clearly.

"I see," he said quietly. "You want romantic dinners and expensive gifts. You want to show me off to your friends and hold hands in public."

"I want to be treated with respect," I said as I closed my fingers into a fist. "I'm not a whore. I'm not going to fuck you because I'm grateful that you want to protect me. I'm not a goddamn damsel in distress!"

He didn't say anything, but his eyes hardened as they swept

over me. "I'll get my security to assign you two men to keep an eye on you. I promise more discretion than the last men showed," he finally said.

I guess I had my answer. I was good for quick ride but nothing more. "Thank you. I appreciate that. If you don't mind, I'm ready to go home now."

He nodded and stood, and I breathed a silent sigh of relief. Had he pushed, even a little, I knew that I would have melted in his arms.

And I wouldn't have even cared if I regretted in later.

CHAPTER EIGHT

Lucas

By the time Monday morning rolled around, I was feeling rough. Sloan stayed in my head all weekend. I wasn't even mildly interested in inviting another woman to warm my bed. At least she'd agreed to the protection detail.

Gripping my coffee like a lifeline, I exited the elevator and walked in on Torrence staring at an unsuspecting Cecilia. She was bent over the desk, fumbling through her papers, and he had a clear view of her cleavage. "Is this really how my week is going to start?" I grumbled as I pushed past him.

"You're late," he snapped in return as he followed me to the office. Startled, Cecilia looked up sharply and immediately blushed. "Good morning Mr. Montgomery. Good morning Mr. Torrence."

"I thought I told you to call me Drew," he said with an easy smile.

"Torrence," I said in a warning voice. He gave her one last

smile before following me into my office. "You should really just ask her out and put me out of my misery," I grumbled as I dropped my briefcase to the floor.

"Who pissed in your cheerios this morning?" he asked with narrow eyes. "I emailed you a detailed background check on Sloan Whitlow. Nothing raised any red flags. I hired two men outside the agency to follow her. They're ex-military, so they should stay out of sight. I also swept all the conference rooms."

I froze and stared at him. I'd only asked him to check one room. If he checked them all, then he found something. "I want signal jammers installed everywhere on this floor. Hell, maybe even the whole damn building. This week."

Torrence shrugged and tossed the little gadget on my desk. "The bug itself is pretty cheap, and it doesn't have much range. I'd say someone would have had to be within two floors of the room to hear anything."

It relieved me to know that it may not have been the board members, but it opened up the pool of suspects to anyone in my building. Only the top floor was restricted. I tipped my coffee mug back and wished desperately it was something stronger.

"Hire whoever you need to help you find the mole. I want it kept quiet, but I want them found immediately."

"Whoever put it there will already know that you found it. We won't exactly be taking them by surprise," Torrence noted. "But it'll be easier to find them if they're nervous. I know of a few guys who could help."

"Someone who will blend in, please. Your poker buddies look like ex-cons." In fact, many of Torrence's contacts were ex-cons, but some were military and a little rough around the edges.

He nodded his head and stared at me for a moment. "Do you really think I should ask her out?"

"Torrence, you're a grown man. Please don't ask me these questions."

"But—"

"Leave," I growled. I sure as hell didn't want to deal with anyone's love life right now. Catching sight of the clock on the wall, I hissed. I had a meeting starting in five minutes.

So much for enjoying my coffee and trying to get my thoughts together. Grabbing my notebook and pen, I tried to clear my mind and pull myself together.

The marketing department had pulled together some new ideas of Montgomery's new line of camping equipment. I'd acquired Galavant Supplies two years ago, but I was just now trying to give it my full attention. Most of the marketing ideas were polished and approved by Steinburg before they crossed my desk, but I liked to make the rounds to all the departments and judge how they were progressing and working with each other.

Walsh met me in the elevator. "Good morning, Mr. Montgomery," he said eagerly. "I've picked up your suits from the dry cleaning and sent flowers to Mrs. Addison for her birthday."

Helen Addison was the only female member of the board, but she was also the most terrifying. Normally I'd made it a point to never forget her birthday in order to stay on her good side, but this year it had completely slipped my mind.

"Thank you," I said gruffly to Walsh. He was irritating, but he was on top of his game.

"There's one last thing," he said nervously. Cecilia has an engagement lined up for you this weekend, and I've been looking at the recent blog posts about you."

I put my hand out to stop the elevator doors from closing. "People blog about me?"

"Oh yes. The average person gets their news from social

media. Anyway, you haven't brought a date with you anywhere in public for the last couple of months. Some are saying that you're hiding a real relationship. Some are speculating that your gay, and a few are wondering if your annual membership to an escort service ran out."

Narrowing my eyes, I glared at him. "Excuse me? All of these rumors are popping up just because I've showed up to one or two events alone?"

"Seven," Walsh said quietly. "You've showed up to seven events alone. I know it's not my place, but you should really have a date this weekend."

I didn't cater my personal life around the whims of the media, but an idea was forming in my head. The more I thought about it, the more wicked it became. "Write this down."

He quickly pulled out his phone and waited expectedly.

"A green dress. Sexy but still appropriate for the function. Have the saleswoman call me when you get there so I can give her the measurements. I'm also going to need a dozen red roses."

"You're going to buy a dress for your date?"

"I'm going to make it impossible for her to turn it down," I said with a sly smile. "I've got a meeting. This is your priority. Do you understand?"

"Yes, sir," he said with a small salute. I snorted as the doors started to close. Just before they shut completely, I thrust my briefcase out.

"Walsh!" I called out.

"Yes, sir?"

"For the love of God, please take Cecilia." He didn't respond, and I couldn't help but smile. Neither one could stand the other, but I didn't trust Walsh to pick out something that wouldn't be completely slutty.

The marketing staff was already assembled on the fourth

floor meeting room by the time I got there. The department was so big that they spanned ten floors and were headed by eight different people. I had everything from ship building to baby supplies under my umbrella, and while each company retained their own marketing team, I liked to know that my own teams were supervising them.

"Good morning. Sorry I'm late," I said as I slipped into the room. The chair at the head of the table was open, and I sat down heavily. "I'm just here to observe, so please continue as though I'm not present."

I said that every time, but I doubted that it had any affect. I'm sure the meeting ran quite differently when I wasn't around.

Someone slid a box of doughnuts my way, and I hesitated before grabbing one. It wasn't often that I indulged, but the sugar rush wouldn't hurt. I snagged a glazed one and settled back. The meeting started, and I aimlessly ran my pen over the paper.

Of course my little wallflower was looking for romance. Most women that I saw wanted more, but none of them dared ever say anything to me about it. In fact, I couldn't remember the last time a woman had turned me down.

"Most of the Galavant products are geared towards men. In fact, in their ten-year history, they've never had a single female in their advertising. I think it's important to portray that the products are tough enough for men and women," the girl said nervously up front. She pointed the remote to the screen at the front and an image appeared.

It was a beautiful woman, clearly a model, hiking up a mountain with a large bag strapped to her back. There wasn't a single strand of blonde hair out of place, and her face was heavily made up. I immediately frowned. I could see where she was going with the idea, but it was all wrong.

"She's too pretty," I said out loud. "The average woman who goes camping will turn their noses up at that image. You want someone who isn't as put together. Someone who doesn't care if her hair isn't perfect. Someone who isn't going to worry about make-up. She's not there to impress other people. She's there to enjoy nature. She's searching for solace and not approval from society."

It was the first time I'd ever made a suggestion at one of the meetings, and a hush fell over the room. I pitied the poor young girl in the front. "It's a good concept. I absolutely want to market equally to both sexes, but we're not selling glamour. We're selling equipment. The idea is excellent. You just need a new model. Someone with long and unruly curls. Someone with soft skin but tough eyes. A genuine smile. No skinny frames or large fake tits. A real woman."

"That's very specific," she said nervously. "I'll start a search immediately."

It was specific. Too specific. Pissed that I'd let Sloan distract me from work, I nodded my head to encourage her to continue. If there was one thing that I prided myself in, it was my focus on the job.

Today I was thinking about her silky skin. The way she'd arched into my touch. The look in her eyes when she'd rubbed herself on my hard cock.

While the meeting droned on, I pulled out my phone and scrolled through the email Torrence had sent me on Sloan.

Both her parents were still alive and living in Washington. Her mother was a school teacher and her father was an engineer. She had no siblings. Graduating at the top of her class, her undergrad professors had given her glowing recommendations to the graduate program. Torrence wasn't wrong. Not only were there no red flags, but there wasn't even a traffic ticket to her name.

She'd lived with Randi Jones for the past two years. There was only one noted relationship. Victor Willis.

I made a note to check out this Victor Willis. I didn't even bother trying to convince myself that it was for the case. I just wanted to know what he was like.

I wanted to see who Sloan Whitlow had said yes to.

CHAPTER NINE

Sloan

My eyes slid over the paper as I mentally tried to rehearse what I was going to say to Dr. Elliot. I had a meeting in an hour, and if I couldn't get him to approve of my paper thesis, I'd be even more behind. As it was, I was already having a hard enough time catching up.

I reached for the cereal, but the box slid across the counter. Frowning, I looked up to see Randi holding it up. "No breakfast until you tell me what happened with your date Friday night. You've spent all weekend avoiding me."

"I've spent all weekend at the library. And it wasn't a date."

"When Lucas Montgomery takes you out on a Friday night, it's a date. I can't believe you're not making a big deal about this. He is the number one hottest bachelor in the city, and he doesn't take women out. Please tell me you climbed on top of him for a nice, long, hard ride. And then give me the details."

"Randi!" I exclaimed as I snatched the cereal box. "Of course not!" Although I still wasn't sure how I'd walked away from him. Every time I closed my eyes, I felt his hands on me. "He just took me out to dinner to convince me that I needed his protection until this whole thing blew over."

"You're not looking at me. When you don't look at me, it's because you're lying. What are you not telling me?" She narrowed her eyes and stared at me. I felt a flush creep up my cheeks, and she gasped. "You dirty, dirty minx. You did do something scandalous with him! Details."

I poured the cereal and shook my head. "There's not a lot to tell. He made it clear that he wanted me, but you said it yourself. He doesn't date. He fucks a woman for a short time and then moves on. I don't do casual relationships."

"You don't do casual relationships because you've never done casual relationships," she said with a sly smile.

Rolling my eyes, I grabbed the milk from the fridge. "I've never done heroin either, but I don't see you making that argument." Taking a bite of my cereal, I immediately spat it out. The rancid taste of the spoiled milk caused my eyes to tear up, and I immediately turned on the faucet and ducked my head under to wash away the taste.

"Jesus," I hissed when my gag reflex finally died down. "When was the last time we went to the grocery store?"

"You were supposed to go this weekend," she smirked. "But you were too busy hiding from me."

"For the last time, I wasn't hiding from you. I was busy."

"Right. Busy. How do you expect to have a relationship with someone when you can't even remember to buy milk?"

"All the more reason for me to stay away from Lucas Montgomery," I muttered, but I already knew what she was going to say.

"All the more reason for you to enjoy some hot and dirty sex with a hot and dirty man. It'll help you relax. It might even help you focus a little better."

I grabbed my paper and shoved it in my bag. If I hurried, I

might be able to grab a bagel from the coffee shop before my meeting. "And just how do you know that he's hot and dirty?"

"Please," she snorted. "Anyone looking at that man can tell that he knows what he's doing in bed. If you don't jump on that, I will."

"Be my guest." We both knew that it was an empty threat. If there was one person I could always count on to have my back, it was Randi Jones. "I have to go. We're not going to talk about this again."

"It's like you don't even know me," she called out as I escaped the apartment.

As usual, I scanned the parking lot for signs of Lucas's men, but if he was still having me followed, they were much better than the first crowd.

Campus was still fairly empty, and I snagged a parking spot close to Professor Elliot's office. With just enough time to spare, I bought a bagel and cup of coffee from the coffee kiosk. Scarfing the plain bagel down, I entered his office breathless and with my mouth full.

"Ms. Whitlow. Good morning."

I swallowed, and smiled. "Good morning, Dr. Elliot. Sorry about the bagel. Spoiled milk."

He frowned sternly. "I have no idea what that means. Please have a seat. I assume that, by your excited email, you have something to show me?"

As I reached for the papers in my bag, the strap slid down my shoulder. When I tried to grab it, I spilled my coffee all over me, and I inhaled sharply. "Shit." Snapping my mouth shut, I immediately colored. It wasn't exactly appropriate to cuss in front of my advisor. "I am so sorry."

"That's all right. You're having a trying month. Why don't you go to the bathroom and clean yourself off while I review the paper?"

Luckily, my paper wasn't soaking in coffee. "Thank you Dr. Elliot. I'll be back in just a minute." Leaving my bag, I hurried down the hall towards the bathroom. The professor had been so patient with me, and here I was acting like a bumbling idiot in his office.

At least he was forgiving.

Throwing some paper towels under the running water of the sink, I started trying to dab at the stain on my red top. Since the shirt slung off my shoulders, most of the coffee hit my chest, and luckily, it wasn't scalding hot.

How did he know that I'd had a trying month?

I froze and stared at my reflection. For a second, I was aware of every sound in the bathroom. The flushing toiled from the men's room on the other side of the wall. The footsteps of people hurrying by the door. My own heart pounding in my chest.

"He's just talking about your paper," I scolded myself. What the hell was wrong with me? I was either shoving the threat on my life from my mind, or I was suspecting everyone who walked past me. There seemed to be no reasonable in-between.

Angrily throwing my paper towels in the trashcan, I threw open the bathroom door and glanced down the empty hallway. "This is all his fault," I said to the stealthy men that I knew had to be somewhere close. "If it wasn't for him, I could actually focus on my school work. I wouldn't be suspecting people who are close to me. I wouldn't be weeks behind on my thesis."

A large man stepped around the corner and leaned against the wall. He regarded me coolly, and there was only one word that came to mind when I saw him. Danger. "You have reason to suspect your professor?" he asked in a low voice.

"No," I snapped. "I have no reason to suspect anyone. I just wish that whoever it was would make their move already so I could go back to my normal life. I'm a graduate student. I don't lust over ridiculously wealthy playboys. I don't get kidnapped by weirdos, and I sure as hell don't have people like you following me around!"

Rather than respond to my crazy rant, he simply stepped back and disappeared around the corner again. Alone, I closed my eyes.

Tell me what you like, Sloan. I'll take you anyway you want tonight. I'll fuck you senseless right across this table. No one will bother us.

Lucas's promise never seemed to leave me. Even angry, paranoid, and alone, my body still responded to the memory of his touch. His breath hot in my ears. His eyes staring into mine.

"I'm not this woman," I whispered to the empty air, but there was no one to convince but myself.

CHAPTER TEN

Sloan

By the time my day ended, I was in desperate need of a drink. Dragging myself from the car, I rubbed my temples and waved half-heartedly to a couple out walking their dog.

There was a large box in front of my door. Frowning, I checked the mailing label. It didn't have one, but it did have my name scrawled across the front. It wasn't heavy. I opened the door and pushed it inside with my foot.

When I got it settled on the kitchen table, I stepped back and stared at it. A box just appears on my door without a mailing label? That sounded like an excellent reason to call the police, but maybe that was because I watched too many crime dramas.

With a pair of scissors, I slowly sliced through the tape. "Please don't be a severed head. Please don't be a severed head," I chanted as I cautiously pulled the flap back and peered inside.

Instead of a bloody scene, I found two more boxes. A long narrow box from Lotte's Florist and a bigger box from Goddard's Women's Boutique.

I opened the florist box first and gasped. Inside were a dozen long-stem red roses with a note. "I would very much appreciate your company to the Harrison-Belle Gala this evening."

There was no signature, but I already knew who it was from. I wasn't big on current events, but I knew of the Harrison-Belle Gala. It was an annual event where the rich mingled and gave away insane amounts of money to a charity of their choice. The Harrison and Belle families both had lost children to cancer, and they'd hosted this event each year. The Children's Cancer foundation was always the headlining charity, but the gala also invited four other charities to join the event. The only person that I knew who was wealthy enough to even get an invitation to the gala was Lucas Montgomery.

Was this an apology? My hands tingled in anticipation as I opened the other box. Inside, nestled in tissue papers, was a beautiful green shimmery fabric. I pulled it gently out by the straps and gasped as the gorgeous dress flowed to the floor.

"So much for saying that I have nothing to wear," I whispered.

There were plenty of reasons I should turn down the invitation. I had work to do tonight. I had class in the morning. Any type of press with me on Lucas's arm would be bad. Simply being near Lucas was bad.

But he had bought me a beautiful and expensive dress. And roses. How could I say no to that?

You just want to see him again.

I pushed the accusation aside and grabbed my phone. "Sloan," he answered in a low voice. "I take it that you got my invitation?"

"I think this counts as an expensive gift," I said with a smile.

"You seem to have an affinity for jeans and t-shirts. I wasn't sure if you had anything appropriate to wear."

"And the flowers?"

There was a pause. "I just thought it would be polite," he said softly.

That wasn't the answer that I was looking for. "Why would you want to take me?"

"I'll pick you up at seven," he said without answering my question. He hung up before I could say anything, and I couldn't help but smile.

Was it possible that Lucas Montgomery actually liked me?

Feeling almost giddy, I put the phone down and held the dress up against me. There were only a couple of hours before seven. It didn't usually take me long to get ready, but I did absolutely have to get some mock classroom questions written up for my Children's Lit class.

Lucas Montgomery was taking me out on a date. Maybe my luck was finally turning around.

He would find a dress similar to the one that I had worn at Randi's birthday. It was the same halter style that dipped low over my cleavage and scooped all the way down my back. It fell to my ankles with a long slit up the side.

I don't know how he'd done it, but it fit every single one of my curves just perfectly.

By the time I'd finished pinning my curls up and applying a little bit of make-up, I stared at myself in the mirror. I could have actually passed as pretty. Stepping into the same heels that I'd borrowed from Randi that first night, I completed the look.

There was a sharp knock at the door, and I took a deep breath. "Here goes nothing," I whispered.

On the other side of the door, Lucas Montgomery looked absolutely immaculate in a black tuxedo. My mouth went dry as

I stared at him. With just a little bit of scruff and those intense eyes, he looked like sin wrapped up in a pretty bow.

"You look nice," he said stiffly, but as his eyes roamed over me, I felt almost complete naked. Exposed.

"You look nice as well." At least my voice didn't crack this time. Gripping my clutch, I stepped outside and closed the door behind me. Rather than one of his expensive cars, a limousine waited for us out in the parking lot.

"I think this was how my prom was supposed to go," I said without thinking.

"Excuse me?"

"The pretty dress and the limousine," I said hastily. "I'm not trying to cheapen anything, but it's the only other formal occasion that I have ever experienced."

"And how exactly did your prom go?"

I gritted my teeth. It was eight years ago and shouldn't still upset me. "It didn't. My date stood me up," I muttered. Dustin Wheeler. He'd been one of the best looking guys in the school, and I'd been speechless when he'd asked me out. In high school, I'd been a joke. I was the bookworm with the frizzy hair. All I needed was the dorky glasses to complete the cliché.

And the handsome football player to humiliate me. That part actually did happen.

"This isn't prom, Sloan," he said as the driver opened the door.

"Of course not. Forget I even said anything," I blushed. Slipping into the car, I berated myself. Already I was sounding like a complete idiot. "Tell me what to expect."

"At the gala?" He sat close to me and rested his arm on the seat behind my head. There were empty seats along the other side of the limo and spots just behind the driver's seat and at the back. Plenty of room to spread out, but his thigh pressed against mine. All he had to do was move his hand an inch, and he'd be touching me. Instead, he seemed completely relaxed and oblivious to how my body was heating up. "The intention behind the charity gala was noble, and the Harrison's and Belle's both strive to keep it that way, but most of the guests don't go to support charity. It's all politics and appearances. But when people are flashing that much money around to impress others, the charities do win out."

"You sound like you don't approve."

"I wouldn't have even gone if it weren't for my board members. The demand that I make certain appearances each year. Since I've turned up solo to all the events in the past few months, I was advised that taking a date would be good for my reputation."

His voice was easy and unconcerned, and I felt my heart drop. Of course this had everything to do with his appearance and nothing to do with me. He'd probably known that I'd be so easy to manipulate.

"I see," I said coldly. I thought about moving to another seat, but I didn't want it to be obvious that my feelings were hurt.

"You're upset." He moved his hand and stroked his thumb down the column of my neck. I knew it was to distract me, but I still couldn't help but warm under his touch.

"It's fine. Do you know how long it will last? I have class in the morning." I leaned down to move away from his fingers, but he simply took advantage and slipped a finger down the length of my spine. I couldn't even help myself as I gasped. "Damn it," I muttered. "Why do you do that?"

"Do what?" His finger slipped under the fabric of my dress, and I immediately straightened and cleared my throat.

"Touch me when I'm angry," I snapped as I wiggled away. Every time he was close to me, I felt all logic fly out the window.

"Do you want me to stop touching you?"

No. Yes. Fuck. "I can't think when you're touching me," I said lamely.

"You're not supposed to think, Sloan. You're supposed to feel. I do have an ulterior motive for tonight, and you should be very aware of it."

My heart fluttered. "What ulterior motive?" I whispered.

He leaned down and kissed my bare shoulder. My eyes drifted shut as his hand skimmed under the fabric of the dress to brush along the side of my breast. "You're not wearing a bra."

Just a little more. I was almost ready to beg for it. Just a little more, and he'd finally be touching my aching nipple. "It's not the kind of dress you wear a bra with." I turned my face to him and desperately hoped that he would kiss me. My lips burned for him, and although he'd already set my body on fire, he still hadn't let me taste him.

He pulled his hand away, and I moaned in frustration. Chuckling, he slid a finger up the slit of my dress. "Is it the type of dress that you wear panties under?"

No. "That's for me to know," I said as I licked my lips. Silently berating myself, I knew that I was playing with fire. We both knew it. Just a couple of days ago I'd told him that I wouldn't be his toy, and here I was, on the cusp of begging to be used.

"That's fine. I have every intention of finding out for myself before the night is over with."

"Lucas!"

"Don't. When the night is over, if you want me to take you home, I will. No questions asked. But I think you're going to want to satisfy your curiosity."

He continued to caress my bare thigh, and I grew wetter by the second. "Curiosity?"

"Just how many times do you think I can make you come in one night?" he whispered in my ear. "From my fingers. From my tongue. From my cock."

Fuck. I was so ready to find out. I wanted to find out right then and there, but the car pulled to a stop. He immediately straightened and gave me a cocky smile. "We're here."

Taking a deep breath, I tried to collect myself, but no amount of straightening my dress could dampen the desire inside me. I knew that I wasn't going to be able to hold him at arm's length forever.

CHAPTER ELEVEN

Sloan

Politicians. Celebrities. Business tycoons. My eyes widened as I took everything in. The wait staff moved with silver trays through the crowd carrying champagne, martinis, and wine glasses. Everyone mingled in the middle, and while they were laughing and talking, none of it looked genuine.

"It's pretty," I said lamely. It wasn't a lie. Someone put a lot of money into decorating the place. The tables lined up along the wall were dressed in white with gold embroidery. Each was decorated with a tall center candle and several smaller candles surrounding it, all in crystal hurricane vases. Lights swooped over the large curtain that hung from ceiling to floor, and right in the middle of the charity booths was a champagne fountain.

"Pretty?" he said with a cheeky smile. "This is thousands of dollars' worth of decorations in here, and all you can say is pretty?"

"To those of us who have never seen thousands of dollars'

worth of decorations, it's pretty." I suddenly brightened. "Do you think Chris Pine is here?" I had a huge crush on Chris Pine.

He rolled his eyes and guided me into the crowd. We could barely take a couple of steps before someone would stop him to talk. All eyes seemed to land on me, but no one asked me for my name.

Maybe they knew I wasn't important. His hold on me never wavered, but as the time passed, I realized that I was no more than a decoration on his arm.

"Montgomery! What is this I hear about you buying real estate in Boston?" one pot-bellied man said as he stretched out his hand.

I felt Lucas tense before he reached out and shook it. "Jackson. I haven't bought any property in Boston," he said with a forced smile. "But I did see the article. I guess someone jumped the gun on that one. I'm fairly focused on the Japan project."

"I see," he said skeptically. His eyes dropped to me, and I decided that enough was enough. "Hi. I'm Sloan Whitlow," I said as I held out my hand.

Lucas looked at me sharply, but the man just smiled and took my hand. His lips grazed across my knuckles and lingered a little too long. "Daniel Jackson, at your service. I own the Surf and Sand resorts."

"Wow. I'm a graduate student."

He roared with laughter and dropped my hand. "A graduate student? That's rich."

Lucas steered me away, and I glanced back, confused. "Why is that funny?"

"Don't worry about it. Would you like some champagne? I see someone that I need to speak with, but you're welcome to help yourself to any of the food and drink. Just don't leave the hotel. I had your security detail take the night off since you're with me."

My stomach growled, and I realized that I was a little hungry. "I'll probably just steal some food and go talk to the people at the charity booths. They look like they're more my speed anyway."

He nodded shortly, but his eyes scanned the crowd. "Pick your favorite one. I'll donate to that one."

"What? I don't think that's how it works, Lucas. You're supposed to donate to the one of your choice. It's not my money."

"They're all the same to me," he said. "I'll be back in a minute."

Aghast, I watched him walk away. They were all the same to him? That was cold.

Wrapping my arms around myself, I made my way through the crowd until I stopped at the Animal Rescue Foundation. Snagging some finger sandwiches from the tray, I offered one to the guy behind the booth. "Hungry?"

A smile broke across his face as he took the sandwich. "Starving. Thank you. Most of the guests here don't pay much attention to us."

"What do you mean? Aren't you here to talk about the charity?"

"I am. I have a whole speech planned out, but no one really ever asks. They just hand me their credit cards and sign after I swipe it."

I studied him. He was close to my age, and while he was dressed in a suit, he was clearly uncomfortable in it. Finally, someone I could relate to. "Well, I'm Sloan Whitlow. Unfortunately, I have no money to give you, but my date told me that he'd donate to the charity of my choice. So by all means, give me your speech."

He laughed and handed me a brochure. "All right. The Animal Rescue Foundation is a hundred-acre sanctuary for domestic and farm animals. We accept any surrenders, no questions asked, and we also rescue animals from euthanasia in kill shelters. Right now we're fostering seven horses, twelve pigs, several birds, close to a hundred dogs and cats, and a camel. Most of our animals are sick or have been severely abused. We charge a small adoption fee, but most of the animals live their entire lives on the sanctuary. Money for food and medical services comes entirely from donations, and our staff is made entirely of volunteers. We don't have to pay anyone in the organization a salary which means that a hundred percent of the donations goes to the animals."

I opened the brochure and put a hand over my chest. The pictures showed a straggly rag-tag group of animals, but they all looked content splayed out on their chewed and torn beds.

"We only have two stables, and both of them are in desperate need of repair. We're also hoping to install a shallow pool to provide therapy for our older arthritic dogs," he said as he pointed to the brochure. His finger slid over my hand, and he immediately reddened. "Sorry."

I couldn't help but smile. He was attractive. Certainly more my speed than Lucas, but I didn't feel the same sizzle. "I think I've heard of you guys. Do you do field trips for the local elementary schools?"

"We do, but we just implemented the program a couple of years ago. You can't possibly be old enough to have a kid in elementary school!"

"No, I'm a graduate student studying childhood development and education. I'm actually working on my thesis, and I came across a list of popular field trip destinations in the area. What do you do with the kids?"

"We try to teach them proper care and responsibility for animals, but I think, to them, we're a petting zoo. The schedule allows them to leash, walk, train, and feed the animals. They get a pamphlet about pet responsibility when they leave."

"Do any of the parents complain that their kids come home begging to adopt a pet?" I asked with a laugh.

"Actually, we get a good percentage of families that come back. They either want to adopt, or they want their kids to help out during the summer. We offer a camp program for kids to volunteer and help out once school lets out."

The wheels in my head were turning. There were no activities for elementary kids in the summer that were connected to the school system, but an organized program where kids could try out and volunteer at a number of places around would both educate and entertain. They could volunteer at animal shelters, soup kitchens, nursing homes, and even hospitals. It would go a long way in teaching them compassion, responsibility, and diversity.

"Do you have any information on your summer program that I could take with me?" I asked suddenly.

"Sure. We're still accepting applications for camp counselors. If you like animals and kids, it'd be a great place for you. It's part time, so you can still work," he said as he bent behind the booth and grabbed a folder. When he stood back up, he immediately paled and looked down.

An arm wrapped around my waist, and I stiffened. Lucas possessively pulled me towards him. "See something that you like?" he asked me softly.

"If you're talking about the charity, yes," I said with narrow eyes. Pulling out of his hold, I took the flyer. "Could you write your contact information on here in case I have any questions?"

His eyes widened, but he grabbed a pen and scribbled on the paper. "Thank you. I will definitely be in touch."

Lucas had a firm grip on my elbow as he steered me away.

"What is wrong with you?" I hissed as I jerked away. "You told me to pick a charity."

"Talk to them. Not get their numbers," he growled. "When you're on my arm, you don't flirt with other men."

Trying to keep my voice down, I glared at him. "You are such an asshole. I wasn't flirting. I think his organization's program could be implemented in schools. Not that you've ever bothered to ask, but it's what I'm busting my ass to study. And if you're not going to actually treat me like a date, I'll talk to whomever I want."

"Not treat you like a date? I bought you flowers and a dress," he said as he stared at me. "I thought that's what you wanted."

"Then you don't know the first thing about me. I came along because I thought this was your way of apologizing to me, but it's obvious that the women you drag around are supposed to be seen and not heard. You should see the surprise on these people's faces when I try to introduce myself. You might as well have picked some whore off the street."

I watched as his jaw clenched with rage, and I took a deep breath. "I'm going to the ladies' room. Don't follow me."

Spinning on my heels, I kept my head up as I walked towards the bathrooms. Tucking the paperwork into my clutch, I turned at the last minute and skirted around the crowd. What I really needed was some fresh air, but I knew he would freak out if he thought I was trying to leave without him.

"Controlling bastard," I muttered as I strode through the lobby and opened the double doors. The cool air rushed to my skin and instantly calmed me. I inhaled deeply and rolled my shoulders.

How mad could I be at him? I agreed to join him tonight knowing full well that all he wanted was a quick roll in the sheets. I had nobody to blame but myself.

I turned to explain to the valet that I was just here to walk around a bit when I realized that no one was at the stand. Dread filled me when I scanned the parking lot.

No security. No people milling around.

The headlights weren't turned on when the van barreled out of the darkness. As it screeched to a stop, I whirled around and ran desperately for the door. I would have made it too if they weren't waiting for me. They stepped from behind the columns and grabbed me. Before I could scream, they shoved something into my mouth.

This time, they were ready for me. Binding my arms with a zip tie, they quickly lifted me and shoved me in the van.

Ten seconds. It couldn't have taken longer than that for me to realize that I wasn't getting out of this one.

CHAPTER TWELVE

Lucas

She was gone. As soon as I burst through the doors of the hotel, I saw the familiar van speeding off. Her clutch lay on the asphalt with the contents spilling out.

Fear gripped me as I pulled out my phone. Torrence grumbled as he answered, but I didn't have time for that. "They have her," I said urgently. "I need a trace on my phone. If they call, I want to know where they are immediately.

"You're at the gala?" he asked, obviously awake now. "Which direction did they go?"

"South down Waters Edge. White paneled van. No obvious markings. I couldn't see the license plate."

"I'll see if I can direct some traffic cameras that way and track them. Call the police, and for God's sake, Montgomery, do not leave that hotel. Don't even think of trying to play hero."

What the hell did he think I was going to do? It wasn't like I could run after them on foot. I had more money than God at my disposal, but at that moment, I felt completely helpless.

Logic told me that they'd try to ransom her first, but all I could see was her mangled body lying on the side of the road. What if this had nothing to do with money? What if they were just sadistic bastards bent on hurting me?

I called Detective Allen before heading back inside to pull the hotel manager aside. "I don't want you to raise an alarm, but there was just an abduction in your parking lot. I've alerted the police, but I want to see your security tapes."

His eyes widened. "Mr. Montgomery, are you okay?"

"Do I look okay? The tapes. Now."

Rubbing his hand nervously, he shook his head. "Should we wait for the police? I really think —"

"I will wire a thousand dollars into your personal account if you'll just shut up and do as I ask."

Money talks. He snapped his mouth shut and nodded his head. "Of course. Our security office is right back here."

The Water's Edge Hotel hosted many expensive private parties each year, so their security was impressive. Monitors covered the walls, and I could see the ball room, the lobby, the bar and elevators, each floor of the hotel.

And the parking lot.

"Rewind the outside feed," I said darkly.

They took one look at my face and bent their heads to comply. Staring at the screen, I felt like someone had punched me in the stomach.

Sloan was practically fleeing the hotel. She'd barely made it down the front steps when two men stepped out from the shadows and shoved something in her mouth. She tried to fight, but they had no problems binding her and tossing her in the van.

"Where the hell is the valet? Your outside security men?" I barked. "Don't you have people out there?"

"Yes, sir." One of the guards picked up the radio and tried to contact the valet station and patrolling security. When there was no answer, I felt my whole body break out into a cold sweat.

"Find them," I said hoarsely. Praying that they were just knocked out instead of dead, I pulled out my phone and gripped it in my hand.

There wasn't a chance in hell that Sloan wasn't going to fight. If they decided that she wasn't worth the trouble, they'd kill her.

Torrence beat the police to the hotel. I wasn't even surprised. Before he could cut the engine, I slid into the passenger seat. "Drive."

He didn't follow the command. Instead, he turned off the car and turned to face me. "She's here."

"Are you insane? I saw them drive off with her. I just watched the security tapes. I will fire you and make sure that you never find work in this city again if you don't turn this car on and start driving."

"Montgomery."

I blinked and stared at him. There was something earnest in his voice. "How can she possibly be here," I finally whispered.

"The traffic cams caught them turning left at every light. Either they're the least organized criminals in the world and turned the wrong way out of the hotel, they're circling back. If it were me, I'd hole up in the one place I knew the police wouldn't be looking."

I shook my head. "There are cameras crawling all over this hotel. They'd never get back out unseen."

He unbuckled his seat belt and climbed out of the car. "I need to talk to security, but I bet the staff uses the tunnels that run under the hotel to get in and out without bothering guests. I doubt there are cameras monitoring them. Stay here and wait for the police. I'll be right back."

As soon as he disappeared into the hotel, I followed him and grabbed the nearest employee. "I'll give you five hundred dollars if you tell me where the employee entrance and exits are."

Her eyes widened, and she nodded. "There is only one that leads out of the ballroom. It feeds directly into the kitchen."

"Show me."

Shrugging, she put down her tray and led me to the hallway with the bathrooms. At the end was a door marked employees only. "How many tunnels lead outside?"

"Just one. It leads into the employee lounge before it breaks off. The maids' offices are down there, and the laundry. It's easy to get lost if you don't know where you're going. The trash receptacles and storage rooms are down there as well. It spans the whole length of the building."

"Are there any employees down there?"

She shook her head. "I doubt it. Most of the staff have gone home, and those of us that are still here won't leave until well after midnight. The cleaning staff is gone for the night."

It was the perfect place for them to take her. No witnesses, a maze of rooms, and the one place the police wouldn't look. "I need you to find a man named Torrence and tell him that I'm down there. He's going to be with security and he's probably going to be pissed. Can you do that?"

She nodded and scurried away. Loosening my bow tie, I took a deep breath and slowly eased the door open. I had no weapon, but if it was money they wanted, I would clear out my bank accounts to save her.

The hallway led directly into the kitchen. I could hear the clanging of pots and pans and the cook shouting orders. All noise ceased and everyone stared at me as I walked through the double doors.

"Don't mind me," I muttered as I crossed the kitchen. "Which door leads to the exit?"

"The one you came in," one girl said timidly. She obviously thought I was drunk and turned around.

"The employee exit," I asked impatiently. "Which door leads to the employee exit?"

Wordlessly, they all pointed to the door on the left. I nodded curtly, and eased it open. Just as I walked into the barely lit tunnel, my phone vibrated.

It was an unknown number.

Answering it, I held it up to my ear and waited.

"We have your woman. If you want to see her again, you'll get two million dollars to us within two hours. Call the police, and she dies," a distorted deep voice ordered.

"You kidnapped her from a public parking lot full of prominent people. Security already called the police," I snapped. "Not to mention that banks are closed. I won't be able to get my hands on that much money until the morning."

There was a pause and some chatter in the background. They'd had at least two weeks to get their shit together, and they were still fucking up. They had to be the dumbest criminals ever.

"Well?"

"We'll call you back." The call ended, and I grimaced. They clearly hadn't thought things through when they decided to hole up in the hotel. What would that mean for Sloan?

Pressing myself into a darkened corner, I dialed Torrence and waited.

"Where the hell are you?" he snapped.

"I just got the ransom call. I don't think they counted on the banks not being open. Get some police to the exit of the hotel. They're going to try to leave with her."

"How do you know?"

"They don't have a choice. If they're still here in the morning, the staff will catch them."

I hung up the phone and waited. The faint sounds from the kitchen echoed into the hallway, but there were no footsteps. I had to get closer to the exit if I wanted to catch them.

The phone vibrated again, and I answered it. "Get the money by ten in the morning. We'll call you then with further instructions."

"I want proof of life," I said immediately, but the call had already ended. "Damn it."

Shucking off my jacket, I rolled up my sleeves and moved cautiously down the wall. Each time I came to a corner, I peered around it, but I was still alone. Worried that Torrence was wrong and they weren't here, I kept following the exit signs.

Just as the girl had said, the last room before the door was the employee break room. I eased the door open and hid just inside the opening. If they were here, and the police were out back, there was nowhere for them to go.

Time blurred. I had no idea whether I'd waited minutes or hours, but a single voice finally echoed off the walls.

"Let go of me you, you fucking assholes!"

There was my proof of life.

CHAPTER THIRTEEN

Sloan

As they dragged me down the tunnel halls, I spat out the rag and started to scream. "Let go of me you fucking assholes!"

"Shut the hell up!" one of them hissed. "Duncan, shut her up."

The fist came out of nowhere and connected to my jaw. Pain radiated throughout my face, but I didn't stop. "If you want me to be quiet, you're going to have to fucking kill me. Who will pay your damn ransom then?" I snarled.

We neared the exit doors, and my heart dropped. If I didn't get free before we left the hotel, God knew what they would do to me. Dropping my body, I let my full weight slow them down. They grunted and reached for me, but before I knew it, they'd dropped me to the floor.

Stunned, I watched as Lucas leapt from an entryway. He'd struck two of the men before the doors opened up and police swarmed the area.

"Sloan," Lucas shouted as he grabbed me. "Damn it, baby. Are you okay? Say something."

He pulled me to my feet, and I just blinked and stared at him. "I didn't know you even knew how to fight," I said softly. "I figured you were the type who paid other people to do that."

"Is that your way of saying thank you?" he said softly. He pulled a small knife from his pocket and sliced through the ties on my wrists. I immediately wrapped my arms around his neck and sagged against him. Now that I was safe, there was no more fight left in me.

That just left fear, horror, and shock.

"You scared the hell out of me." As the police surrounded us and people barked orders, he finally lowered his head and kissed me.

Hot. Desperate. Urgent. This wasn't the hesitant first kiss. I could taste fear, anger, and desire wrapped all in one. For a moment, he chased the demons away, and I returned the kiss with fervor. He may not be the forever kind of guy, but he was here now.

When I grew too dizzy and breathless, I had to break the kiss. Burying my head in his chest, I ignored the buzz around me. I didn't want to talk to anyone. I just wanted to be alone.

"Can she talk to you tomorrow? I don't think she's ready to give a statement," he said in a low voice.

"We've got paramedics here to check her out."

The voice sounded familiar. I pulled back and looked into the kind eyes of Detective Allen.

"I'm fine," I muttered quietly. "I just don't want to be here anymore."

He nodded. "Take her home. I'll give you both a call in the morning."

Lucas wrapped his arms around me and slowly walked me through the doors. I turned my head and watched the flashing blue lights. I'd seen them far too much lately. Just past them, the limousine was waiting.

I slid inside and huddled in the corner. Lucas sat across from me, and I wondered why he wasn't touching me. Why he wasn't holding me.

"My bag," I said hoarsely. "My bag is still inside."

"My head of security has it. It'll be returned to you," he said in a low voice. There was something dangerous and restrained in his tone. "Do you want me to take you to your apartment?"

Randi would be there. She'd want to comfort me. She'd want to talk to me. I wasn't ready for that. Numbly, I shook my head.

"Where do you want to go?"

Turning away from him, I rested my head on the window. I had no idea where I wanted to go.

I STARED OUT THE WINDOW. The moon hung high over the acres of the Montgomery Estate. I should have been exhausted, but I think I was still in shock.

"Sloan, do you want something to drink?" Lucas asked softly. He hadn't said much of anything in the car. There was a dark rage that swirled in his eyes, but he was gentle as he helped me from the car to the house. Even now, I could hear the anger simmering just under the surface.

"You're angry," I said softly without turning around.

"Do you want a drink," he asked again.

"Sure." I didn't really, but it would give me something to do.

I heard the click of the cabinet and the distant sound of running liquid. His reflection appeared behind me, and I held my hand out. The glass slid in my hand, and I gripped it automatically. "Thank you."

Raising it to my lips, I sipped slowly at it. "Your place is nice."

"What the hell were you thinking, Sloan?"

There it was. The accusation that was written all over his eyes. I knocked the rest of the bourbon back and sat the empty glass on the table before I turned to stare at him. "I was upset and needed some fresh air. There shouldn't be anything wrong with that," I said softly.

"You knew that I'd pulled your detail because you were with me. You knew that no one was watching you when you left that party," he hissed.

Something inside me snapped, and I narrowed my eyes. "So this is my fault? What was I supposed to do? Spend the rest of my life under your protection?"

"At least you would have been safe!" he roared. He dropped his glass and let it shatter against the floor as he grabbed my arms and pushed me up against the window. "The minute I realized that you were gone, I thought I'd gotten you killed."

His body pressed up against me, and I realized that he wasn't angry at me. He was angry at himself. "Lucas," I said softly as I reached up and touched his face. "You didn't kidnap me. This isn't your fault. You can't blame yourself."

"You do," he said through clenched teeth.

"I don't." A storm raged inside him, and was terrified to think of what he would do if he continued to carry the guilt on his shoulders. "I blame the men that kidnapped me. I blame myself for letting my feelings cloud my judgment. The one person that I do not blame is you. And it's over now. They're never going to touch me again."

"It's over," he echoed.

"We can both go back to our normal lives. You don't have to worry about me anymore." My pulse spiked as I spread my hands over his chest. "It's over, Lucas. The night is almost over."

His eyes darkened as he pressed his body harder against mine. "It's not over until I say it's over," he growled. "You should have gone home, Sloan."

I lifted my chin and stared at him. The memory of the night's events was blurring, but I remembered his lips on mine. It was the only thing that had shaken me from my fear.

"I didn't want to go home."

"Tell me no, Sloan. Tell me that you don't want me. You should have someone gentle, and I don't think I can be gentle tonight."

I should have. I should have done all those things, but the only thing I truly wanted was for someone to chase the fear away.

I wanted to feel good.

Hooking my arms around him, I took his hand and slid it up the slit of my skirt. Higher until he could feel the heat pulsating from my pussy.

He groaned and rubbed his thumb across my wet lips, and I jumped at the pleasure that cascaded through my body. I knew that if I did this, nothing would ever be the same, but my life had changed the minute he'd touched me at the club.

I didn't have the strength to do what was right. I wanted to do what felt good.

"I need you," I whispered, and I dropped my inhibitions.

Tonight, my body would be his.

To be continued...

BOOK TWO: WHEN HE CRAVES

DESIRE. EROTICISM. BETRAYAL

The threat to Sloan Whitlow was over, but her relationship with Lucas Montgomery is just beginning. Despite her misgivings about the multi-millionaire, she can't deny her desire for him. When he offers her an arrangement where they can enjoy each other, she agrees on one condition.

HE CAN'T BE with anyone else.

LUCAS KNOWS he has no reason to keep the intriguing woman by his side, but he isn't ready to let her go just yet. After one taste, he knows he has to have more. He agrees to be with her and only her, but his history is no secret, and she doesn't trust easily.

IT WAS ONLY SUPPOSED to be a casual relationship. Their passion rivals only their tempers, but when the professional threat against Lucas, turns personal, he might lose her forever.

CHAPTER ONE

Sloan

"Tell me no, Sloan. Tell me that you don't want me. You should have someone gentle, and I don't think I can be gentle tonight."

I should have. I should have done all those things, but the only thing I truly wanted was for someone to chase the fear away.

I wanted to feel good.

Hooking my arms around him, I took his hand and slid it up the slit of my skirt. Higher until he could feel the heat pulsating from my pussy.

He groaned and rubbed his thumb across my wet lips, and I jumped at the pleasure that cascaded through my body. I knew that if I did this, nothing would ever be the same, but my life had changed the minute he'd touched me.

I didn't have the strength to do what was right. I wanted to do what felt good.

"I need you," I whispered, and I dropped my inhibitions.

Tonight, my body would be his.

. . .

His lips were on my throat as he hiked the fabric of my dress up to my waist and slowly inserted a finger inside me. Leaning my head back against the glass, my eyes drifted close. My body had been waiting for this the moment I'd laid eyes on him, and now that it was here, I thought I might explode before we'd even begun. Unable to help myself, a low moan escaped me.

Lucas hissed at the sound and raked his teeth across my skin. "I've dreamed of the sounds you would make when I pleasured you. When I fucked you," he muttered. "Everything about you makes me so goddamn hard."

He added a second finger and stroked deep inside me. My legs weakening, I had no choice but to wrap my arms around his shoulders and try to hang on as he continued to wreak havoc on my body.

"Lucas," I whispered. "If you don't stop...I'm going to...God, we haven't even started...please..." I panted, but when his thumb circled my sensitive nub, I lost all control. Burying my head in his shoulders, I cried out as my body convulsed around him. I was embarrassed by how easily my body had responded to him and upset that it was already over.

Suddenly, his hands swept under me and easily lifted me in the air. When he laid me down on the bed, I took a deep breath. He'd obviously keep going until he'd found his own pleasure, and I needed to prepare myself. It had been rare for my ex-boyfriend to make me come before he'd even entered me, but when it did happen, sex was almost painful.

"Sloan," he said in a low voice. "Why do you suddenly look upset? Do you want me to stop?"

"No," I said with a forced smile. "I can handle it."

His face was full of concern as he leaned over me and slowly stroked my cheek with his finger. "Baby, I know I said that I might be rough, but I'm not going to hurt you. If you're not ready, we can stop."

It was sweet of him to give me an option, but I wasn't going to stop just because I had some issues with sex. "I want to keep going. I'm just a little nervous. It's been a while."

"You look more than nervous, my sweet. Let me see if I can make you feel more at ease." There was a wicked look on his face as his hands slid up my thighs and pulled my dress up. I lifted my hips and then my back and shoulders as he slipped it off my head. Completely naked and feeling vulnerable, I tried to cover myself, but he quickly pinned my arms to the side.

His eyes darkened considerably as he gazed at me. "Let me see you, Sloan. You have no idea how badly I've wanted to see this. God, you are absolute perfection."

There was something in the way he looked at me, but I felt my body warm despite my hesitation. He let go of my wrist and trailed a hand down my throat and over the swell of my breast. I arched against his touch and felt my body reawaken.

"You like that?" he asked softly as he bent down. "What about this?" Running a tongue over my erect nipple, he pulled another deep moan from me. Before too long, I was bucking against him. I desperately wished he was naked, but I couldn't help rubbing my pussy against the cock still restrained in his pants. "It seems that you do."

His head slid down my body as he licked a path to my sex. I saw his intentions, and quickly grabbed his head. If he fucked me with his tongue, I'd come again, and I wouldn't have anything left to give him.

"Please," I muttered as I forced his head up. "Just fuck me. I'm ready."

Lucas's eyes narrowed. "Did you just deny me?"

"I'm ready, Lucas. Please. I'm ready for you."

Sliding off the bed, he began to unbutton his shirt. "Touch

yourself," he demanded hoarsely. "I want to see you touch yourself."

My cheeks reddened. I had never done that in front of anyone. When I didn't quickly follow his command, his hands stilled. "Sloan. Do it. Touch yourself."

Afraid that he'd stop and I'd never feel him inside me, I slowly moved a hand down my body until I could lightly strum my clit. There was something forbidden about having his eyes on me while I played, and it only made me hotter. My hips twisted under my touch, and I bit down on my bottom lip. "Please," I whimpered. "Please hurry."

"You can stop." He stood naked by the bed, and every fantasy in my head hadn't even come close to reality. Every inch of his skin seemed to beg for my touch. Hard sculpted muscles, skin smooth and taut. His erection was, to say the least, impressive.

He covered my body with his and kissed me with a desperate urgency. As I spread my legs, his erection rubbed against me until I could take no more. "Lucas," I begged. "Fuck me. Now. Please."

Without another word, he slid inside me with a grunt and immediately stilled.

God. He stretched and filled me, and I gasped.

"Sloan," he hissed. "Hold still. Let me have a minute."

I froze under him and closed my eyes. I'd never felt anything like it. "Are you...?"

"Not yet," he hissed. I saw the sweat forming on his forehead. He was straining to stay in control and not push the rest of his cock inside me. Slowly, I rocked my body just a little. I liked the way he felt, and I wanted all of him.

"Fuck, Sloan," he moaned. "Baby, you have to stop. You're too tight. I don't want to hurt you."

"Don't hold back. I can take it. I need you." I couldn't stop even if I wanted to. The more I rocked, the deeper he slid until he released a guttural moan and lifted my knees as he finally sank all the way home.

Wrapping my legs around his waist, I leaned up and licked the sweat from his skin as he started to pump his hips. Although he tried to be slow and easy, we were too far gone for that. Soon, he was hammering inside me.

Flames licked my body as the tension grew inside me. I wanted to touch and kiss him, but I could do nothing but let him control me, twist me, and move me as he pleased. When he sucked my breast into his mouth and flicked his tongue over the nipple, I arched helplessly under him. Sex had never felt like this before, and I was almost afraid to climax.

Gasping and panting, I gripped the bars of the headboard and held on to it as it slammed into the wall.

Faster. Deeper. I was so close. "Lucas," I whimpered. "I'm going to come. Fuck. I don't know."

"I've got you," he moaned. "Come, baby. I want to feel you around my cock."

He covered my mouth with his and swallowed my scream as I lost all control of my body. Growing almost rigid under him, I tightened my legs around his waist in an effort to keep him inside me as I careened over the edge of chaos. My toes curled, and my nails dug into his back. I'd leave marks, but he didn't seem to care.

"Fuck. Sloan. Ah, God," he moaned as he suddenly slammed hard inside me and grunted. I felt him spill his seed until finally, he slumped over me, nothing but dead weight and complete and utter satisfaction.

I didn't give a damn how heavy he was. As I tried to catch my breath, I traced my fingers over his back like an old lover familiar with every curve of his body.

Finally, he lifted his head and stared at me. "You want to tell me what the hell that was?" he asked accusingly.

Surprised, my eyes widened. Why was he mad? "What do you mean? Is there something wrong with me?"

"With you?" he laughed hollowly. "Your body is nothing but an addiction waiting to happen. But I wanted to taste you, and you stopped me. Why?"

Embarrassed, I tried to wiggle out from under him, but he kept me trapped. "Sloan," he said warningly.

"I don't usually orgasm more than once," I admitted finally. "It can make sex a little uncomfortable for me."

A slow smile spread across his face. "Ah, baby. You are so sweet and so innocent."

He rolled us over until I was sprawled out on top of him. As if on instinct, my legs fell apart and I straddled him. His hands immediately started to stoke my side and ass. I couldn't even believe it as I started to grow wet again. He dug his finger into my ass cheeks and slowly forced my body to slide over him.

"You don't ever have to worry about that," he whispered. "I'll train your body to be wet just by my mere presence. A single word. A memory."

I shivered and stared at him. Was that the kind of woman I wanted to be? At the mercy of a man who could make me wet with a single word? It troubled me, but I couldn't stop my body's reaction. He stirred and hardened, and I couldn't help but shake my head.

"You're ready?" I whispered. "Again?"

"And that's my problem with you," he hissed. "I'm always ready for you."

Before I could decide what to do with that, he slid inside me and chased away all my logic.

When he touched me, stroked me, kissed me, and filled me, I couldn't deny him anything. I was his.

CHAPTER TWO

Lucas

I stood at the large windows of my office and looked down below. The city continued as if nothing had happened. Cars sped along the streets and honked angrily at each other. People scurried back and forth, desperate to reach their destinations in time. Everything was the same as yesterday and the day before.

Except for me. I was hardly the same. The object of my desire had been in my bed all night, and I'd thought my obsession would finally abate. Slake my desire, and I'd be able to satisfy my curiosity.

Sloan was gone the next morning. She'd slipped out of my bed after only a few hours of sleep and asked my driver to take her home. She hadn't even said goodbye.

It was rare that a woman voluntarily left my bed. Rarer even still that a woman didn't call afterwards for round two.

I don't know if it was my pride or my confusion that kept me from calling her. Even after slating my desire twice in one night, she was still on my mind. She hovered about in my dreams. She flitted across every thought.

Sloan controlled my body even when she wasn't there. It was maddening. Even worse, I couldn't help but suspect that she didn't feel the same.

"For the love of God, Montgomery, your secretary has been calling you for five minutes. What the hell is wrong with you?"

I turned suddenly to see Howard Steinburg, my vice president, frowning at me from the doorway. Annoyed that Sloan was once again keeping me from work, I forced a smile. "Sorry," I muttered. "A lot on my mind."

"When the hell were you going to tell me that there was a bug in the conference room?" he growled. His face was red with anger. Steinburg was pushing retirement age although he never discussed stepping down. I always had the feeling he'd keel over from a heart attack before he let that happen.

"I'm trying to keep it as quiet as possible," I said mildly as I sat down.

"You should have told me."

"I don't have to tell you anything." My voice was low and hard. Although I hated to do it, sometimes I had to remind Steinburg that he worked for me and not the other way around. He was a brilliant businessman, and I paid him an obscene amount of money to work for me, but he was a man of control. I knew he thought of me as a son, and he only bothered me when he also thought of himself as a boss.

My boss.

There was an awkward moment of silence before he visibly relaxed. "Damn it, Lucas. Don't you trust me?"

"It had never even crossed my mind that you would be a mole." I leaned back in my chair and cocked my head. "But you were focusing on a major overhaul in the legal department, and

I didn't want to add this to your work pile. Torrence is handling it. This is why he works for me."

Steinburg narrowed his eyes. "Torrence was hired to head your security department. Since when does that extend to investigating?"

"Torrence has many talents." I rocked gently in my chair. It wasn't really the time or place to go into Torrence's abilities.

"Fine," he grunted and slumped into the chair. "And what is Torrence doing about it?"

"Narrowing down the pool of suspects. I'll let you know if there is anything worth telling. Was there any other reason you decided to storm my office?"

"This kidnapping business that happened over the weekend. The woman is all right?"

The woman was driving me insane. "She's fine," I muttered.

"And you have no idea who the perpetrators were?"

I rolled my shoulders. "The detective called me yesterday. Their bank accounts showed that someone paid them, but they're not talking. They'd rather rot in prison than reveal the name of whoever paid them."

"You think someone might try again?"

"They'd be a fool," I retorted. "My security is far too vigilant for that."

"Any idea why they targeted the woman? She could have been involved. Prey on your weaknesses for pretty women. Take a cut of the money."

Anger surged through me, but I kept a lid on my temper. Sloan was a weakness that I was not ready to admit to just yet, but I sure as hell didn't want anyone suspecting her of anything. She was completely innocent. In more ways than one. "She was researched at length. Torrence and the police have cleared her of any wrongdoing."

"So you're done with her?"

I heard the underlying suspicion in his words. "What exactly are you asking me, Steinburg? You've never given a damn about my private life before," I said softly.

He studied me for a few minutes before shrugging. "I don't give a damn. Your father never let personal relationships get in the way of his success, and I'm sure you won't do the same."

Snorting, I shook my head. "I own an international company, Steinburg. I've already achieved success."

"Don't think it can't be taken from you, my boy. Even Rome fell in a single day."

I looked at him sharply as he rose, but I couldn't decide if he was threatening me or warning me. "I'm sure she'll be thrilled to know you think she has that much power."

"I don't think she has that much power, Montgomery. I just know how much power a man can give when they're thinking with their cock instead of their head," he said coldly. "The company is a success because you are always in complete control."

He wasn't wrong. I enjoyed women quite frequently, but my thoughts never strayed past morning. At work, I was focused. At night, I could play.

"Is that all?" I said with great restraint. This wasn't a conversation I was prepared to have.

He shifted uneasily and nodded. It was obvious that he had more to say but was afraid to push the envelope. Instead, he rose and smoothed a hand over his shirt. "Keep me informed, Montgomery."

"If I feel that's necessary, I will." I didn't bother getting up or showing him to the door. I didn't care if it was rude. I was unhappy with his accusations, and I wanted him to know it.

When I was left alone with my thoughts, I couldn't help but replay the scene again in my head. Steinburg wasn't one to overstep his bounds often. Just what had gotten into him today?

I asked my secretary, Cecilia, if she could page Torrence to my office. There had been some heavy flirting between the two of them lately, but I tried not to concern myself with it. Torrence was a hard man to love, and while Cecilia had love to give in spades, her main focus was always on her kids. So if she wanted to indulge in some harmless flirting at work, it wasn't my business.

Half an hour before my next meeting, Torrence entered the office. Tall and broad, Torrence had a few visible scars from his time in the military and perhaps twice as many invisible scars. He was a rugged and hardened man with a dark past, but I trusted him with my life.

He'd worked for my father for several years before I hired him, and although I considered him a friend, his past was so classified that I couldn't even begin to investigate it. Not that I would.

If there was one person that I trusted in this world, it was Drew Torrence.

"You rang," he said with a yawn as he walked in. Plopping himself on the couch rather than the chair, he groaned and rolled his head around.

"Long night?" I asked dryly.

"Long weekend. It wasn't easy getting information about your would-be kidnappers from the detective and even harder trying to figure out what the hell happened. These aren't professionals who are maintaining their loyalties. They're so amateur that if I held a gun to their heads, they'd piss their pants. Whoever they are protecting scares the shit out of them, and that's never a good thing."

I leaned back and frowned. "You think this plot to extort money from me and the mole are connected?"

"I think there isn't enough information about either to come to any conclusions. One would definitely distract you from the other, but the only other way I can see a connection is if the mole wanted to blackmail you for money. If that were the case, I would have thought that we would have heard something by now. How's the woman?"

"Sloan is fine," I said shortly.

"She spent the weekend with you."

Taking a deep breath, I shook my head. "She spent one night with me."

Drew narrowed his eyes and studied me for a minute before bursting out laughing. "My God, man. It bothers you that she didn't stay the weekend. What happened? Did she slip out without saying goodbye and now your feelings are hurt?"

"Don't be ridiculous," I snapped angrily. "A one-night stand is just fine with me."

"So Steinburg storming out of your office and muttering that the woman had you by the balls has nothing to do with Sloan?" I shot him a startled look, and he smiled coyly. "Cecelia knows all."

"Steinburg needs to keep his fucking mouth shut. I've made him a rich man, and he needs to keep his opinions out of my personal life. And Cecelia needs to —"

Torrence held up his hands and interrupted me. "Whoa. Easy, boy. Take a breath and check that temper. If you piss Cecelia off, she'll leave and your life will be in shambles. You wouldn't be able to find your arm pit without that woman, and you know it. If Steinburg is concerned, he's not wrong. You need to get your personal life in order before it affects your professional life."

"My personal life is in order," I said icily. "I wanted her. I had her. End of story."

"So you don't plan to see her again?"

The right answer would have been, yes. I had no plans to see her again. The honest answer was that if she walked through the door right now, I'd bend her over the desk and slide into her sexy little body until we were both breathless. "If the urge arises, I won't deny myself the pleasure of having her again," I said finally. "What's the next step in identifying the mole?"

"I'm sweeping for bugs everyday, but nothing new has shown up. I have the PR department scouring for information about you on the web, but nothing has turned up. I'm still looking through your employee's finances, but frankly, it's a long process. Until they try again, I don't have a whole hell of a lot to go on."

How ironic was that? "I would prefer if we found them before they leak any more sensitive information."

Torrence rolled his eyes. "Thank you for pointing out the obvious. If I could wave my magic wand and produce them before that happens, I would. I told you from the beginning that this could be a lengthy process. You need to be careful with what you say in the conference rooms and don't ever have a meeting before I can sweep for bugs. Ideally, we'd search the board members as well."

"You know I can't do that."

"I know that. You want secrecy, and I'm trying to keep a low profile, but you're playing a dangerous game, Montgomery. You may have to decide between keeping things a secret and protecting your business. It's probably just someone trying to make an extra buck by spying for another company. If they're spooked, they'll probably stop, but you're taking a great chance."

I studied him. Despite his words of warning, he was practically falling asleep on the couch. "Last week you were chomping at the bit over this. Now you're unconcerned."

"Last week I was pissed because you weren't sharing information. Now that we're on the same page, I'm thinking a little more clearly," he said with a shrug.

"Excellent. I'm so glad you're thinking clearly," I muttered sarcastically. "Get back to work."

"You're awfully cranky for someone who got laid this weekend," he chuckled as he stood. "Maybe you should figure out a way to make it more of a regular occurrence."

"Out," I ordered. "And stay away from my secretary!"

His laugh followed him all the way out, and I shook my head. Still, his words rang in my head.

If quenching my desire for Sloan kept me levelheaded, maybe I did need to find a way to see her on a more regular basis. Eventually I would get tired of her.

Women rarely kept my attention for long.

CHAPTER THREE

Sloan

The day was absolutely beautiful. I tried to bask in the sun's warmth as I looked over my textbook. Campus buzzed with life with students rushing to and from class, students laying out on the dorm lawns, and several games of Frisbee and tossing footballs, but these weren't the things that kept me from studying.

After an hour of trying desperately to read about cognitive recognition in adolescents, I wasn't even pretending to look at the book.

I had all but begged for him. I'd been a mess in his arms, and I couldn't stop thinking about it. What the hell had happened?

I tried to tell myself, once again, that I wasn't this woman, but I was starting to sound like a broken record. Maybe I wasn't the woman who fell for complete strangers, got kidnapped, and had mind-blowing sex a month ago, but I certainly was now.

"Hey!"

I looked up sharply to see Randi bouncing my way. Her dark skinned glowed under the sun's rays, and her hair was absolutely perfect as it flowed down her back. She looked absolutely gorgeous in a pink halter-top and a pair of jeans that clung to ever curve.

I, on the other hand, was burning to a crisp with my curls pulled into a pony-tail. In jeans and a blue t-shirt, I looked like a complete bum next to her.

As she closed the distance between us, I thought briefly about pretending that I was running late, but I knew that look of determination on her face. She was out for information, and she wasn't going to let me go until she got it. "You have been gone all weekend. What is going on?"

I closed the book and tried to give her an innocent smile. "Hi, Randi."

"You're about to lie to me. I can already tell," she said dryly. "Your cheeks are already reddening, and you're biting your lip. You're a horrible liar so you might as well save yourself the trouble and tell me the truth."

"I've been in the sun, and my lips are chapped," I said defensively, but I was about to lie to her.

"Sloan!"

"I slept with Lucas," I said quickly. Once the words were out of my mouth, I felt a weight lift from my shoulders. I didn't even know I was dying to tell someone until just now.

Randi clapped excitedly. "It is about time! Tell me everything. Was it amazing? I bet it was amazing."

"It was...nice," I said breathlessly. "It was more than nice. Trust me when I say that Victor was never like that. I just don't know what I'm supposed to do now."

My friend frowned and studied me. "Sloan, I know it's been awhile for you, but you can't fall for a man just because he's good in bed. This is Lucas Montgomery we're talking about."

"I know," I said as my shoulders slumped. "He's way out of my league."

Randi quickly slapped me in the arm. "No. You don't ever say that, and it is certainly not true. You are worth ten of him. But he's not the man for you, Sloan. Lucas is the kind of guy you have a couple rolls in the bed with, enjoy immensely, and then walk away from. He's a playboy, and if you let feelings get involved, you're only going to get hurt."

I guess it was something that I had known all along, but hearing it said out loud was so harsh to my ears. "You're right. I've never done a casual relationship before. What exactly am I supposed to do now? Do I call him? Do I wait for him to call me?"

"You absolutely wait for him to call you. He's probably used to women falling all over him. It will do him some good to work for what he wants."

My ears burned with embarrassment. Had I just been another woman who had fallen all over him? It certainly didn't take me very long to give into his seduction. "I should just walk away and never think of him again," I muttered as I leaned over to shove my textbook back into my bag.

"Sweetie, are you okay? I know it's not your usual thing, but casual sex can be pretty rewarding. Of course, if you have feelings for him, it would be disastrous. You should definitely walk away." She cocked her head and studied me, and I tried to smile.

"I don't have feelings for him," I said with as much conviction as possible. "But he is distracting, and I'm too far behind in my thesis to indulge myself."

I could tell that Randi didn't believe me, but she didn't say anything else. She started chatting about her weekend, and I tried hard to pay attention. As usual, she was the freest person I had met. She lived life with absolutely no fear and no regrets. When she finally gave me a hug, it was tight and comforting. "I'm here for you," she whispered.

As she walked away, my phone vibrated in my pocket. Pulling it out, I glanced at it and felt my blood run cold.

It was Lucas.

I willed myself to ignore it and push it back into my pocket, but just before my voicemail picked up, I answered it.

God, I was weak.

"Hello," I said softly.

"Ms. Whitlow," he said in a low voice. "I thought that you might join me for dinner tonight."

Ms. Whitlow? So we were back at that again. "Lucas, you've seen me completely naked. Please don't call me Ms. Whitlow again," I growled.

"Good to hear your temper is still intact. I'll pick you up at seven."

"I did not agree to go out with you," I snarled. "This is what you do. You just assume that you're always going to get your way. You didn't even actually ask me out to dinner. You just said that I wanted to join you for dinner. Why don't you try asking me for once?"

There was silence on the other end, and I thought he'd actually hung up. "Lucas?"

"I'm suspicious that you're setting me up just so you can have the pleasure of denying me," he said finally.

"Would it really be so bad if someone turned you down once in a while?" I muttered.

Lucas cleared his throat. "I don't want you to turn me down."

I had a feeling that was the closest thing I was ever going to get to a confession of any sort out of him. "Seven will be fine," I said finally.

He didn't even bother to say goodbye as he ended the call, and I rolled my eyes in annoyance.

But I did feel a little lighter as I picked up my bag. Lucas

Montgomery wanted more than just a one-night stand. Something about that felt very good.

By the time he'd picked me up, I had once again gone through every piece of clothing in my closet. Part of me wanted to raid Randi's closet, but I wanted this date to finally be about me. Not about protecting me. Not about using me for the media. Just about me.

I chose a pair of black pants and a simple blue top. It was filmy enough that I hoped it was sexy but it didn't reveal any cleavage.

"Classy," I whispered as I stared at myself. "It's classy."

Sure. Maybe if I said it one or two more times, I'd start to believe it.

He was prompt. Always prompt. I opened the door right at seven and tried not to drool. He just got sexier every time I saw him.

His eyes slowly raked over me. "Hello, Sloan."

"Lucas," I whispered. "Thank you for the dinner invitation. I didn't think you'd contact me again. I figured that since you didn't need to protect me anymore, you wouldn't feel obligated to hang out with me." Hang out with me? Could I sound any more immature?

"Tonight isn't about your protection," he said quietly. "I'm sure you already figured that. Come on. We'll be late for our reservations."

He kept a hand on my back as he led me to the car. I was surprised to see that his driver, Danny, wasn't present.

"You drove?" I asked as he opened my door.

"I like to drive." There was no other explanation, and I slid into the car.

"I assume that you've been busy with your paper, and that's why you slipped out of my bed without saying goodbye." He didn't even bother looking at me when he started the car, but I heard the accusation in his voice.

He wanted an explanation. I latched onto his excuse. "Yes. Study, study. That's me."

"Have you recovered from the incident?"

I'd barely even thought about. No nightmares. No residual fear. Memories of my night with him consumed me.

"Yes, thank you. It helps me to stay busy."

The conversation was strained and polite, and we soon lapsed into silence. I was already regretting my decision to dine with him.

When he pulled into Chateau Jean-Paul, I breathed a sigh of relief. A public restaurant that hopefully had no secret level that afforded couples more privacy and intimacy.

Being alone with Lucas was dangerous. Being intimate with him again would be worse.

"Relax," he whispered in my ear as we walked into the restaurant. "Tonight we'll eat like everyone else."

When I did relax, he chuckled but didn't remove his hand.

Conversation at dinner was just as tense as the car ride. I hid frequently in my wine glass and behind my food. When the bill finally came, I looked forward to leaving. The ritzy restaurant was his world, but I was too busy trying to not embarrass myself that I couldn't even enjoy the food.

There were times when I thought Lucas had lust in his eyes, but it wasn't often. I started to think that maybe I was wrong. He seemed cool and controlled. I couldn't help but wonder if this date was to remind me that we were from different worlds.

That would be for the best, but that didn't stop my heart from pounding painfully in my chest. I grew so anxious that my hands visibly shook when I picked up my wine glass to finish it.

"Are you all right?"

"I'm fine," I muttered. Maybe it was the three glasses of

merlot, but I decided that hiding wasn't the answer. If I wanted to know what he was thinking, I would have to ask. "Actually, I'm not fine. I'm not sure why you invited me out tonight."

He smiled slowly. "Why do you think I invited you out?"

Clearly, he wanted to play one of his games. "You know what? It doesn't matter. I think we can both agree that tonight is just not working. So thank you for the meal and the wine. You can clear your conscious of guilt."

"You think I feel guilty?" he chuckled. "If I seem quiet to you, it's because I'm trying to gauge your state of mind. There is something that I want to discuss with you."

"Oh yeah? And what's that?"

"I enjoyed spending the night with you, Sloan. I think you enjoyed yourself as well."

My eyes widened, and I felt my stomach twist. Where the hell was this going? "Lucas!"

"I'll compensate you for your time, of course. I know it's valuable."

Freezing, I stared at him. "I'm sorry. What exactly are you saying? You want a repeat?"

"Don't you?"

"And you're going to pay me for it?"

"Compensate."

For a half a second, I had no idea how to react. I just blinked. "My God. You're serious." The anger hit me like a brick wall, and my jaw dropped open. "I will not be paid to service you!" I hissed.

He just raised an eyebrow. "You didn't enjoy our night together? I think your multiple orgasms would suggest otherwise."

His voice was a little too loud, and I glanced around nervously. "Lower your voice," I growled. "What I enjoyed is not the point. You're like a drug, and drugs are not good. They're fun for a few minutes, but then there's hell to pay afterwards. I have too much going on to deal with this, and I am not a whore. Take me home. Now."

Trying to keep my composure, I got up and smoothed a hand over my hair. Squaring my shoulders, I held my head high. Of all the nerve! Did he think that just because I was a poor student, I would whore myself out for him?

I left him sitting at the table and prayed that he wouldn't be so angry that he wouldn't take me home.

I was a poor student, and I didn't exactly have money for a taxi to take me across the damn city. Of course, using my credit card and digging myself deeper in debt might have been preferable to riding home with a man who wanted to pay me for sex.

CHAPTER FOUR

Lucas

"You're upset with me," I murmured as she inserted the key into her door. She hadn't said a word as I drove her home, and I wasn't sure what exactly I'd done to warrant the cold shoulder. I wrapped my hands around her waist and felt her stiffen.

"I told you how I felt," she said stiffly. "I'm not some gold-digging whore that's going to be at your disposal whenever you want."

She opened the door. I had a feeling she planned on slamming it in my face, so I followed her quickly inside. When she whirled around, there was fury in her eyes. "I did not invite you in," she hissed.

Shutting the door with my foot, I pushed her hard against the wall and slid my hands up her side until my thumbs brushed under her breasts. She pissed me off, but God did she turn me on.

"At no point did I ever call you a gold-digging whore," I growled. "The problem with you is that you insinuate too much.

Why can't you just take my word instead of reading between the lines?"

"Take your word?" she hissed. "Be at your beck and call and you'll make it worth my time? Just how exactly were you planning on paying me for my services?"

She may have been angry, but she was slowly arching into my touch. "Just because I was going to compensate you for your time doesn't mean you're a whore. I have connections, Sloan. I can accelerate your career path. I can get you in touch with anyone you need to finish your thesis. I can help you."

"You're an idiot," she said through gritted teeth. "It doesn't matter if it's money or not. It's payment for sex. That's what a whore does. If you didn't want a relationship, all you had to do was say so. I'm a big girl, Lucas. I can take it."

Despite the fury in her eyes, I saw the flame of desire. Her pupils dilated, and her breasts heaved. She wanted to fight, but she also wanted to fuck. And I was hardening with every breath that she took.

Leaning down, I kissed her hard. The time for talking was over. I didn't want to hear another word come out of her mouth unless she was begging me to fuck her. She didn't even bother pushing me away. Wrapping her arms around me, she just pulled me closer and reached for my pants.

I let her fish out my hardness and wrap her hands around it. As she squeezed, I moaned and rested my forearms on either side of her. Smiling coyly, she started to stroke me. "Is this what you were going to compensate me for?" she mocked.

"Damn it," I hissed. Pulling out of her grasp, I whirled her around and shoved her against the wall. She automatically bucked her ass against me, and I smiled. "You can talk all you want," I muttered. "But you want me."

"I can want you and still be pissed at you," she grunted and pushed against me again. She looked over her shoulders and narrowed her eyes. "Just like you want me despite your anger."

I wanted to pull her pants down and take her hard against the wall right then and there, but that wouldn't teach her a lesson. I knew exactly what she was trying to do. "You think that because I want you, you can control me?" I hissed as I pressed the palm of my hand to the apex of her thighs. "What happened to the naive woman in my bed not days ago? The one who didn't know could have multiple orgasms?"

"She's thinking a little more clearly now," she snapped, but her eyes were already closing as I pressed my fingers against her.

She moaned softly and rubbed herself on me. Even through the fabric of her pants, I could feel her heat. "God, Lucas," she panted. Suddenly, she slapped her hands against the wall. "I think you're the one trying to control me through sex."

Unbuttoning her pants, I slid the zipper down and peeled them slowly them down her legs. As I bent to my knees, I felt completely at her mercy as I gently ran a finger down the black lacy edge of her panties. We could talk about control all we wanted, but I was hers, and she didn't even have to touch me to prove it.

Fuck. It pissed me off to no end.

I ripped her panties down and turned my body so I could slip my head between her legs and the wall and press my lips to her. She practically screamed as I dragged my tongue across her slit and tasted her.

She couldn't seem to help herself as she rubbed her wet pussy across my tongue. Her legs quivered in my hands until my hold on her was the only reason she was still standing, but I didn't let up. I flicked my tongue over her clit until she cried. I shoved my tongue deep inside her until she whimpered, but when I could feel her close to her release, I let up.

"Lucas," she moaned. "Please."

"Please what?" I hissed as I looked up at her. She rested her forehead against the wall, and her hair spilled down her shoulders.

"Please let me come," she whispered. "Please."

I blew gently against her until I had her squirming, and I finally raked my teeth lightly over her clit. Her whole body shuddered as the climax ravaged her body, and I loosened my hold as she slid down the wall. Pushing my body up, I leaned back and let her fall right onto my lap, her legs straddling me.

She blinked and stared at me. "That doesn't prove anything," she whispered as she slowly moved across my erection. Lifting my knees, I worked my pants the rest of the way down.

"It proves that you want me. And you can have me, Sloan," I murmured as I tucked her hair behind her ear.

Her eyes searched me. "Why can't you just call it a relationship?"

The word bit sharply into me. There were relationships with women, and then there was a relationship to one woman. I had plenty experience with the former but virtually none with the latter.

And I wasn't about to start now.

Rather than answer her, I simply lifted her until I could slide into her. She welcomed me snugly, and I grunted as pleasure swept through me. She knew what I was doing. I could see the accusation in her eyes, but need drove us both. Instead of pushing the issue, she just lifted her shirt and unsnapped her bra so that her breasts swung free. As she rode me, I leaned over and took a nipple in my mouth.

I was addicted to every sound of pleasure. The more she moaned, the more I wanted to hear her moan. She moved faster, her pussy stroking me, her body slamming against mine. I dug my fingers into her hips and urged her on.

"Shit, baby," I hissed. "You feel too good. I can't hold on much longer."

She whimpered, and I knew that she was close. Digging my heels into the floor, I pushed my body against the wall until she took me so deep that I didn't know where I ended and she began. The contact was too much for her, and she arched her back rigidly and exploded around me.

As her muscles clenched and milked me, it was all I could do to hold her up as I reached my own climax. Moaning her name, I emptied everything inside her. All that I could give was hers.

When she slumped against me, I closed my eyes and held her. I didn't know if minutes or hours passed, but she finally pushed herself up and stared at me. "We should probably move before Randi gets home," she whispered.

"I'm not leaving," I said darkly as I anchored her to me. "I don't give a fuck if your whole apartment complex walks in on us. I'm not done with you yet."

She laughed dryly and shook her head. "I just meant that we should move this some place more private, like my bedroom. It has a door that locks."

Sloan slowly eased off me and grabbed our clothes. She didn't even look back as she led me to the bedroom, and I felt a little relief when she locked the door behind me.

"It's going to be hard to slip out of your own bed before morning," I remarked as I slid my shirt off. She stiffened and turned to face me.

"You're really not going to let that go, are you?"

"Not until you tell me why."

She tossed the clothes on the floor and shook her head. "I shouldn't have to. I've had exactly one sexual partner, and we were in a long relationship. I'd just had a one-night stand with a man I barely knew. I didn't know how to act."

"It's not a one-night stand anymore."

"It's still a casual relationship, and I don't know that I can do that." She sat on her bed and brought her knees up to her chest, effectively covering her nakedness.

She looked so innocent and vulnerable. I could barely look at her. Sweeping my gaze around the room, I tried to find some answers. The white walls of apartments were so sterile, and the neutral carpeting didn't help. Her color scheme was safe. Grey and white. There were a few pictures here and there, but no bold works of art on the walls. With the exception of her desk, it was meticulously neat. Clothes were hung, her shoes were lined neatly on the walls, and there was nothing strewn about on her dresser.

Her desk, on the other hand, was a clusterfuck of books and papers. It was the first time I could say something concrete about her.

She was a walking contradiction. Quiet and organized. Bold and passionate. Innocent and naive. Seductive and dangerous. If I had any sense, I would have walked away right then.

I kept my voice even despite the knot growing in my stomach. "So tonight is it, then?"

"I didn't say that."

Good. Even though I knew it was wrong, relief swept through me. I walked back to the bed and slowly crawled towards her. Pulling her ankles down, I moved up her body until she could do nothing but lie back as I settled my weight on top of her. "So what are you saying? You want romance? Flowers, jewelry, candle-lit dinners?"

"Yes."

Fuck. I gritted my teeth and shook my head. "I can't give that to you, Sloan. I'm just not that kind of man. I don't want marriage or kids. I can't look past today. But I can show you exactly what your body is capable of. I'll let you act out your fantasies on me and explore yourself."

Her eyes darkened, and I smiled. She was hooked. "Would you be monogamous while we were together?"

I chose my words carefully. "I don't usually use the term monogamy because I don't do relationships. But I know that your last boyfriend cheated on you, and I can only assume that it's a sensitive point for you. If it will help you, I won't be with anyone else while I'm with you, but I can't pretend this is more than a sexual experience."

She never broke eye contact while she considered the agreement. Wordlessly, she nodded. Placing the palms of her hands on my shoulders, she pushed until I flipped us over. Giving me a quick kiss on the mouth, she slowly slithered down my body, her tongue trailing down my skin, until she poised hesitantly over my cock.

The thought of her sucking me off already had me stirring. When she didn't move, I wrapped my hands gently in her hair and tried to tug her back up. "You don't have to do anything you don't want to do," I whispered.

"No, I want to. My ex said I wasn't very good at it." She glanced at me uncertainly. "I just thought that if you were going to let me explore, I could practice."

Nothing in the world would have made me turn down that offer. "Take your time," I muttered hoarsely. Leaning back, I closed my eyes and waited.

She was tentative at first. A tongue from base to tip. A few gentle squeezes. A quick lick at the tip.

It was more erotic than if she'd taken me all the way down her throat. I grunted and tried to keep my hips still while she played.

"Is that okay?" she whispered.

"Oh yeah," I muttered hoarsely. She was going to be the fucking death of me.

When she finally wrapped her lips around me and slid

slowly down my cock, I moaned and couldn't help thrusting ever so slightly into her mouth.

As she grew more comfortable, she took more. Bobbed her head faster. At that moment, I would have done absolutely anything she asked me.

"Sloan?" I finally grunted through gritted teeth.

She used her tongue to play with me as she slid her mouth up and over. "Yes?"

"Your ex-boyfriend is a goddamn idiot."

CHAPTER FIVE

Sloan

This time, when I woke up next to him, I didn't leave. After playing with his body until late in the night, I'd slept soundly next to him, curled around his body like I'd spent countless nights with him. He had one arm thrown around me, and he actually looked peaceful as he slept.

I moved my fingers softly through his hair and tried to figure out what I was doing. I had just agreed to a casual sexual relationship. It felt a little empowering to take control of my sexuality.

"You look a little too pensive this morning," he murmured as he stirred and stared at me.

"I thought you were asleep," I said with a smile. Rather than pulling away from me, he held me closer to his body.

"Tell me what you're thinking."

Turning in his arms, I pressed my hand against his naked chest. He looked damn good in the morning. There wasn't a doubt in my mind that I looked a hot mess. "I was thinking about our agreement."

"Planning on backing out of it now that you're happily satiated?"

I saw the question in his eyes and smiled. "No. I was just thinking that it feels kind of freeing."

"Oh really?" His hand reached down to stroke my naked nipple. My body responded to him immediately. "What do you want to do next?"

I knew what he was asking, but I wasn't quite ready to voice any of my fantasies. "I want to get ready for class so I'm not late."

He groaned in frustration as I reluctantly pulled out of his grasp. "You're supposed to be at my disposal. What if I say that I want you to spend the day in bed with me?"

Chuckling, I reached for my clothes. "I'll remind you that you have a multi-million-dollar company to run. You probably don't have time to spend a weekday in bed."

"That's true. You'll come to my bed tonight?"

Tonight? I so desperately needed to work on my thesis tonight. "I'll try. I've got some research to do, but I'll come afterwards."

"You'll be at the library?"

I nodded as I pulled on a pair of jeans and a t-shirt. His eyes never left me as I pulled my frizzy hair back into a pony-tail. "You keep spending mornings with me, and you'll stop wanting me in your bed."

He whispered something so softly, that I wasn't even sure I heard him correctly.

That's the idea. Is what it sounded like.

Turning sharply, I stared at him. "What did you just say?"

"Nothing."

Taking a deep breath, I turned back to the mirror. He was staring at me, but there wasn't any guilt in his face. Even if he was trying to tire himself of me, it didn't matter. I hadn't questioned his motivations before I made the agreement, and I had no reason to question them now. "I have to go if I'm going to grab some coffee and breakfast before my first class," I murmured as I turned from him. "If you could sneak out without Randi seeing you, that would probably be best."

He slowly stood. As the blankets fell away, I couldn't help but stare. Lucas Montgomery was magnificent. He looked even better in my bedroom. "Are you ashamed of me?"

Snorting, I rolled my eyes. "I doubt anyone would be ashamed of you. I just don't want her drooling all over you. Would you please put some clothes on?"

Moving up behind me, he wrapped his arms around me and met my eyes in the reflection. "Does my nakedness bother you?" he asked huskily.

"Oh no you don't!" I danced out of his reach and shook my head as I grabbed my bag. "I am off to class, and you will quit trying to distract me." I took one last second to drink him in before I slipped out and closed the door behind me.

"There you are!"

I whirled around and stared as Randi stumbled in. Dragging a hand through her hair, she gave me a tired look. She still wore the same pink halter and jeans from yesterday.

I stifled a smirk. "Walk of shame?"

"Why is there no coffee in the pot? There is always coffee in the pot," she moaned. "Did you sleep in? Why did you sleep in? Sloan, I need coffee."

"I did sleep in," I said as I slowly moved from the door. Praying that Lucas would keep quiet and sneak out without Randi knowing, I tried to gracefully leave.

"What did you do last night?" she asked as she cleared her throat. "Christ, I need a shower."

"Just worked on my paper. I am super late, and yes, you really do need a shower. You should take a nice long hot one," I said loudly, hoping Lucas would get the hint.

"Yeah, yeah, yeah," she muttered as she shuffled down the hall. Glancing at the clock, I gritted my teeth.

I was going to be so late.

It was a fact that my professor didn't let slip. When I finally arrived at class, he stopped the lecture and turned to stare at me as I tried to slip unnoticed into class. "Ms. Whitlow, so happy that you could join us," Dr. Elliot said dryly.

"Sorry professor," I said as I ducked my head. Every head in the class turned.

"Would you like to tell us what caused you to miss over half the class today?"

I thought about telling him I was wrapped in the arms of a gorgeous man. But I just smiled briefly. "Alarm clock didn't go off." Quickly sliding into the nearest empty seat, I pulled out my notebook and tried to focus. As Dr. Elliot continued to lecture, I tried desperately to focus. By the time class was over, I realized that I hadn't heard a single word.

"Ms. Whitlow. Do you have a minute?" Dr. Elliot called out as I packed my bag at the end of class.

"Of course," I said with a tight smile. At least he was waiting for the rest of class to leave before he raked me over the coals for my tardiness. Mentally cursing Lucas and all his temptations, I slowly made my way down to him. "Dr. Elliot, I am sorry I was late."

"Ms. Whitlow," he said as he held up his hand and smile. "You're almost never late, so don't think anything of it. I reviewed the information you emailed me last weekend, and although it's very late in the game, I think, my dear, you finally have your thesis statement."

My eyes widened, and I grinned. Over the weekend, I had emailed him the information I gathered from the charity in the hopes that I could include the information in my paper. The need for a summer schedule for students that included both education and pleasure that also taught the kids responsibility and charity. "I can make it work, Dr. Elliot. I know I can."

"You're weeks behind. You'll still have to find a group of subjects to participate and get in touch with the charities to come up with a lesson plan before the end of the semester. You have a lot of work to prepare for," he said warningly.

I nodded eagerly. "I will. I'll get started right away!"

He waved his hand to dismiss me, and I gripped my bag and raced to the library. If I skipped lunch, I had a solid four hours to work before my next class. After that, I could work all night.

Sleep was overrated.

It wasn't until the sun had set and I'd spent hours in the library that my phone vibrated. Frowning, I picked it up and glanced at it.

Your class let out hours ago. Where the hell are you?

My heart sank. I had completely forgotten that I'd told Lucas that I'd try to meet him.

I'm so sorry. I got caught up in researching at the library. I'm going to have to take a rain check.

He texted back almost immediately.

So we make an agreement, and you break it the first chance you get?

What was the big deal? It was one night, and he knew how important my thesis was to me. I said I was sorry. I'll make it up to you.

He didn't text back, and I tried to sink back into my work. I couldn't help but glance at my phone every now and then to see if I had missed his text.

I didn't.

The library didn't close until two in the morning, so I quickly lost track of time. It wasn't until a shadow passed over me that I looked back up again.

Lucas stood over me, and there was nothing but cold anger in his face.

"What are you doing here?" I hissed in a low voice. Looking around, my heart sank when I saw that the library still had a handful of people in it. "How did you even get in here? It's supposed to be student IDs only."

"I have money, Sloan. You'll find that gets me just about anywhere." He sat down and stared at me expectantly.

"You still haven't told me what you're doing here."

"I wanted to see you. We had plans, remember?"

I glanced at my watch. It was nearly midnight. "Lucas, I'm sorry that I forgot, but you can't just sit here and stare at me while I work."

"Why not? I don't stand people up," he said loudly.

Rolling my eyes, I gritted my teeth. "Lower your voice," I snapped. "People are here to study. Are you going to be an idiot every time something like this comes up?"

"Do you expect to stand me up often? If you had called me and told me that you needed to work, I'd be much happier. Instead, you forgot. I don't like being forgotten," he said casually. He did lower his voice, but not by much.

"For fuck's sake," I growled and slammed my book shut. There was no way I was going to get work done now. Shoving my books inside my bag, I stormed out. Predictably, he followed.

Once outside, I whirled on him. "Is this what's going to happen every time I piss you off? You're going to stalk me on campus and embarrass me in front of my peers? I have put a lot of money and effort into my education, and this thesis is going to get me a career! A career that I am working damn hard for. I'm sorry that our plans slipped my mind, but I am weeks behind everyone else, so researching and writing thesis is my main priority. And if your ego can't take that, then you might as well find some other woman to be your stupid fuck buddy."

I turned to continue down the stairs, but he reached out and grabbed my arm. "Do not walk away from me, Sloan," he said in a low voice.

"Let go of me." Fury fueled me as I turned around to stare at him. "Let go of me, now."

His anger matched mine, but he relented and released me. I shook my head as I stared at him. "Do you always throw such a temper tantrum when things don't go your way? How does anybody stand to be near you?"

His face fell, and I worried if my words were too harsh. "Sloan," he said in a low voice.

"It was one mistake, Lucas. I know that I should have said that to you, and I know that you don't love that I forgot, but I can't guarantee that it's not going to happen in the future. You have the right to be upset, but if you got caught up in a meeting, I wouldn't storm into your office and throw a fit." Taking a deep breath, I turned my back on him and moved slowly into the darkness. When he followed behind me, I stopped.

"I'm just making sure that you get to your car safely," he muttered tersely. "I'm sure campus security is not up to my standards."

Controlling bastard. Too tired to argue with him anymore, I let him follow me back to my car. I didn't make eye contact or say anything to him as I slid in the driver's seat and slammed the door shut.

I still felt his eyes on me as I started my car and drove away.

A measly twenty-four hours later, and we'd blown it. Lucas Montgomery wasn't the type of person who forgave mistakes, and I wasn't the kind of woman who could be pushed around.

Despite my convictions, I couldn't help but feel the tears prick my eyes. We were over.

CHAPTER SIX

Lucas

I rocked back and forth in my chair and stared dumbly at Torrence. He kept talking, but I didn't hear a word.

I had seen Sloan annoyed at me. Frustrated. Pissed. But this was the first time I'd ever seen her truly angry.

It was irritating. She stood me up. What right did she have to be mad at me?

"Are you listening to anything I'm telling you?" Torrence snapped.

Rubbing the back of my neck, I yawned. "I'm tried, Drew," I muttered.

"For you to call me Drew, you must be tired. I don't suppose you had Ms. Whitlow in your bed last night?" he asked dryly.

Cocking my head, I stared at him. "Actually, I did not. She's quite angry with me. She think's I'm controlling."

Torrence snorted. "That should not be news to you. You are a controlling bastard."

"She said I threw a hissy fit."

"I think I might actually like her," my friend said with a smirk. "What did you do?"

"I didn't do anything," I growled. "She stood me up, and I just went to find her!"

He stared at me. "Seriously? You stalked her because she stood you up? That's a little over the top."

"Shut-up. Why are you here?"

"I'm trying to give you a report of my findings. I've done a pretty thorough financial background report of nearly a third of the staff, but, while there are some kinky people working for you, I haven't found any strange activity that indicates any payoffs."

"Damn." I rubbed a hand over my face and closed my eyes. Last night, I didn't leave campus right away. I'd walked around a little bit and tried to remember my own time at college.

It was brief. Only two years. I'd only gone because my father demanded it, but college never suited me. I wasn't the partying type. I was raised to be disciplined and in control, but college was full of temptations. My father was furious when I dropped out, but he was dead less than a year later. I wouldn't have finished college anyway. It was strange to me that it would be so important to her.

More important to her than me.

It was a ridiculous thought. She worked hard for her education. I liked her because of that. She wasn't a vapid individual that let her whole life fall to the wayside because a man showed her interest. She had a goal in life that was more than just having a good time. She had substance, and I adored her for it.

Until, apparently, it got in the way of what I wanted.

Damn it, I was a controlling bastard.

"Montgomery! I swear, if I'm just wasting my breath, at least let me know so I can grab a cup of coffee while you put yourself together."

"I'm listening," I growled. "I can sum it up in one sentence. You haven't found the traitor. How is that helpful to me?"

Torrence shook his head and stood up. "You're a damn ass today. Apparently someone telling you the truth really pisses you off. So she thinks you're controlling. Montgomery, you are controlling. That's not a horrible thing. You've built an empire on discipline. Don't beat yourself up over it. If she upset you, find another woman."

I didn't want another woman. I wanted Sloan. And even more strange, I wanted Sloan to like me.

The revelation startled me. I normally wanted women to lust after me, and that was never a problem. Sloan definitely lusted after me. Her body responded to every touch. Every word. But I never cared if women liked me before.

"How long will it take you to finish your search?" I asked finally.

"At least another week," he sighed. "Maybe longer. I know you have a board meeting tomorrow. I think you should postpone it."

"If I postpone it, I'll have to give them a reason why. Just because we don't think it's a board member doesn't mean it's not. I have to pretend everything is normal."

"The traitor knows you found their bug. It's not like you have to hide from them," Torrence pointed out.

"But if I take too many precautions, they might do something more drastic. As long as we sweep for bugs before the meeting, it should be fine. If any information leaks, then we'll know it's a board member. I'll just have to be careful about the information I share," I said finally as I turned to stare out the window.

"Montgomery, I've looked at the financials of the board members. If one of them is the mole, they're doing it for personal reasons. Have you done anything to piss them off lately?"

"They've invested money in me, but it doesn't mean that I listen to every word they say. I run this company as I see fit, and that doesn't always sit well with them. But I can't think of anything that I've done lately," I muttered. Hamburg brought the traitor to my attention, but that didn't immediately exclude him. Addison had been in a generous mood since her birthday, but I had a feeling that had more to do with the lover she kept on the side than with me. Holmes kept to himself, and Jenson was young and pompous, but his seat on the board gave him status. He wouldn't jeopardize that just because he was angry with me.

"I'll watch what I say in the meeting, Torrence. Don't worry. Even if the company crumbles at my feet, I have enough money in the reserve to keep you employed," I said dryly.

"Idiot," Torrence muttered. "I don't even know why I try to be your friend. You should take this more seriously."

"Trust me, I take it very seriously." And personally. Someone was trying to take me down. I took that very personally. "Keep up the search. Let me know what you find."

Torrence nodded and opened the door. "Iris?" he asked in a surprised voice.

Iris? I whirled around to see the gorgeous blonde standing in the door with a smirk on her face. "Hello, Drew. It's been awhile," she said, but her eyes were on me.

"I thought you were in Europe."

"I was. I just got back. How have you been?"

Torrence looked uneasily over her shoulder at me. Iris and I had a brief relationship, but although it lasted only a few months, it was much longer than any other woman had held my interest. I was happy with our arrangement, but she had left suddenly for Europe and never said a word. Just disappeared one day. It wasn't until I started snooping around that I realized she'd left the country. I never contacted her, and she'd never contacted me. "I'm fine. It's good to see you."

He slipped past her, and Iris looked at me expectantly. "Well? Can I come in?"

Warily, I nodded. Iris was always calculating. Her return was not without reason. "What can I do for you?"

"So formal," she chuckled as she walked in. I was relieved to see that she left the door open. "I thought you'd be happier to see me."

"You didn't exactly say goodbye before you left."

She sat on the couch and crossed her legs. Her short blue dress rode high along her thigh, and she lounged seductively. "We both know it didn't bother you, so there's no need to pretend it did. I warmed your bed at night, and that's all you needed. Or were you just upset because I left you before you could leave me?"

Iris had a point. I walked around the desk and leaned against it. "What can I do for you, Iris?"

"Nothing professionally. I'm back in town, and I thought you might have some free time."

Her meaning was clear, but I wasn't interested. "I'm sorry Iris. I've got a lot going on right now."

"I've been in town for a while, Lucas. I've heard rumors that you're showing quite a bit of interest in a pretty young thing. A student. Now why would you have interest in a student? You normally like more powerful women. Experienced women."

Stiffening, I felt a sudden urge to defend Sloan. Protect her. "So you're jealous?"

"Not jealous. Just curious." She trailed a finger up her thigh.

Cocking my head, I stared at her. "Just how long have you been back, Iris?"

"About a month. Long enough to hear about the kidnapping attempt. Long enough to know how publicly distraught you were when the girl disappeared. Long enough to hear about your daring rescue."

And long enough to plant a bug in my company. "A month, and you didn't reach out to me before?" I asked casually. "What exactly was your business in Europe? Pleasure?"

Iris was the daughter of a wealthy oil tycoon. Although she didn't need to do anything with her life, she had a head for business, and her father frequently asked her for advice. She wasn't some naive woman. She was a strategist, and if she thought she could use me to further her rise in the business community, I had no doubt that she would do it.

"I spent some time on the topless beaches of France. Lounging in the cafe's of Italy. Flirting with the handsome men of Greece. It was a nice vacation. You should have joined me," she said with a coy smile.

"You should have invited me." My voice was cold. There was no way she spent months vacationing in Europe. Iris got bored if she had nothing to do for an hour. Weeks of lounging would have driven her insane.

She stood and walked towards me, swaying her hips. Iris was a natural beauty. Curves in all the right places. Gorgeous even without a stitch of make-up. Tall and leggy. She knew she was captivating, and she utilized it like a weapon. "If you missed me, Lucas, I'd be more than happy to make it up to you."

She tried to reach for me, but I clasped her wrists before she could touch me. "If I were you, I'd be very clear about your intentions, Iris. Your true intentions. I'm a busy man, and I don't like games."

The smile slipped from her face, but before she could say anything, someone cleared their throat. Looking up sharply, I saw Sloan staring at me from the doorway. Her face was a mixture of anger and jealousy.

"Sloan," I said in a controlled voice. "This is Iris Norwood."

I tried to stay as calm as possible. Iris would, without a doubt, try and rile Sloan, and our relationship was too fragile for that. I pushed Iris slightly back before releasing her hoping that she would take the hint and move back even more.

She didn't.

Sloan walked in slowly. Her eyes locked with Iris's. "Norwood? The oil company?"

"Yes. Who are you? Lucas and I were discussing something quite intimate before you interrupted us," Iris said with a mocking smile.

Damn it. "And our conversation is over," I quickly intervened. "Iris, you don't need to come back."

She looked sharply at me, and there was surprise in her eyes. Whatever she thought of my relationship with Sloan, she clearly didn't think it would trump my relationship with her.

"Fine," she said stiffly. She cast another look at me before sweeping past Sloan.

"Sloan, what are you doing here?" I asked softly.

"You came to my campus. I thought that it was only fair if I came to your work," she said as her head turned to stare at the door.

Great. She was still angry. "Sloan, this isn't a good time. You also distinctly pointed out last night that storming my office wasn't something that you would do."

"I didn't storm," Sloan muttered. "I would have waited patiently with your secretary, but your door was open."

I clenched my jaw and took a deep breath. There was nothing in her body language to indicate why she was here. "Could we speak later? I'm a little busy right now."

As soon as her eyes met mine, I knew I'd said the wrong thing. There wasn't fury or anger in them but suspicion. She crossed her arms and cocked her head. "I'm sorry. I definitely didn't come here realizing that I was going to interrupt you and the gorgeous woman that used to decorate your arm and your bed."

Fuck.

CHAPTER SEVEN

Sloan

"Shut the door," he said in a low voice. He moved around the desk and sat in his chair. The new distance between us didn't make me feel any better.

I did as he asked, but I had a feeling that I was quickly losing control of the situation. I had just walked in on him touching another woman. It wasn't in a sexual manner, but I could see the intentions in her face, the disgust in her face when she walked past me.

"Why don't you tell me what you're doing here before one of us says something we regret?" he asked softly.

The door shut with a soft click, and I turned to face him. My heart was racing. "I came to apologize."

"Really?"

"Yes, so imagine my surprise when I find you in the office with your ex-girlfriend," I hissed. There was no way I was just going to let that pass.

"I told you that I wouldn't fuck anyone else," he said darkly as he stared at me. "I haven't. Why don't you trust me?"

I didn't break eye-contact. "It did occur to me that you were under the impression that I broke our agreement last night."

"If that were true, I could fuck whomever I wanted."

Pain sliced through me, and my eyes widened. I couldn't say anything in response to that.

"She showed up unannounced at my office. I had no intentions of doing anything with her. When our agreement is over, you'll know."

His controlled fury sent shivers down my spine. "I'm sorry," I whispered. "You've just been with so many women, and she's so pretty."

"Come here."

His voice left no room for argument. I slowly moved from the wall and shuffled to him. My heart hammered against my chest. I had no idea that he could be so angry.

I stopped in front of his desk, and he shook his head. "No. Come here."

Shit. Swallowing hard, I moved around the desk and stood in front of him. I wasn't scared of him. Deep down, I knew that he'd never physically hurt me. I wouldn't be here if I thought that was the case, but I still had no idea what he was going to do.

His hands moved to the button of my pants, and my eyes widened. "Lucas," I hissed and tried to swipe his hands away. "We're in your office!"

"My office. My business. My building. My rules," he snapped. "You're free to walk out, but if you stay, you're going to listen to me."

"Listening doesn't usually require the removal of my pants," I whispered, but I didn't stop him again. There was something thrilling about fucking him here. I'd tentatively asked Victor if he ever wanted to fuck me in the car, but he'd always brushed me off. It turned out that he was fucking other women in his car, but that wasn't the point. This was my chance to do something really daring.

But he was just so angry.

Reaching back, I gripped the edge of the desk behind me, and he slowly unzipped my pants and pulled them down. Underneath, I wore a flimsy piece of lavender lace that dared called themselves panties. I'd gotten in the habit of wearing sexy underwear whenever I thought I might see him.

"She is beautiful," he muttered, but he never took his eyes off my pussy. Gripping my hips, he lifted me easily on the desk and rolled his chair between my legs. "And I've had her."

Damn it. I didn't want to hear about him and other women. "You don't have to explain."

"Oh, I know I don't," he said as his eyes met mine. His finger trailed up my inner thighs, and I hissed and curled my toes. "I don't have to explain a damn thing to you, but you should trust me. When I tell you that I won't be with anyone when I'm with you, then you need to trust that. When this is done, Sloan, you'll know."

"Okay," I whispered.

"Not okay." He pulled the scrap of fabric to the side and shoved a long finger inside me. It took me be by surprise, and I fell back. Catching myself on my elbows, I accidentally shoved papers off the desk. Neither of us even paid attention as they hit the floor. I gasped as pain mixed with pleasure.

"Lucas?" I asked uncertainly.

He stood suddenly and leaned over me to kiss me hard. Pushing a second finger inside me, he started sliding them in and out. "This isn't what I do, Sloan. I don't just be with one woman. I take whomever I want home at night without a second thought. I'm putting in the effort to hold my end of the bargain. The least you could do is trust me."

The tension built inside me, but I tried to ignore it. "Lucas, I'm sorry."

His thumb pressed against my clit, and I fell all the way back and planted my heels against his desk as I bucked against his hand. He kept talking. "You knew of my past before we agreed to this. I can't change any of that. You're going to have to be okay with that."

If he wanted me to respond, he was going to be disappointed. I could barely moan as he continued the assault on my body. Hard and fast. Slow and easy. His fingers were driving me wild.

When I felt his hot breath blowing on me, his tongue sliding across me, sinking inside me, flicking my sensitive clit, I lost it. Distantly, I hear the clatter of something heavy hitting the floor as I searched for something to hold on to, to anchor me while my orgasm threatened to fling my body into oblivion.

He never let go of me. When it was finally over, he slowly pulled my limp body off the desk and into his lap as he sat back down. "I'm sorry," I whispered into his shoulder.

Gently, he kissed the top of my head. "I think I kind of like your jealousy," he said. I heard the smile in his voice. "But if you're not careful, it'll push us to the breaking point. I'm enjoying you, Sloan. I'm not quite ready to let that go just yet."

Neither was I. Of course, the difference was that eventually, he would be ready to move on.

And I might never get to that point.

"How did you know that Iris was my ex?"

"I Googled you," I muttered as embarrassment stained my cheeks. "There are quite a few pictures of you with women on your arm."

"Don't do that, Sloan. If you can't be at peace with my past, then you need to tell me now. And if you can, then you can't dig up old bones."

Wordlessly, I nodded. He was right, of course. The only thing that would do was upset me. "I should go."

I tried to get up, but he didn't move his arms. "I owe you an apology for last night. You're not wrong. I am used to controlling the environment around me, and I have a short temper. In the future, I will try to be more understanding of your other obligations."

Smiling, I turned my head to stare at him. "Lucas. I never expected you to be a man who apologizes easily."

"I'm not. Now go on. I'll see you tonight."

I stood from his lap and felt a little empty without his arms around me. "I can't. I have several meetings tomorrow at the local school so I can pull together a group of kids for my thesis. I have to work on my notes."

For a moment, I thought he'd be upset, but he just smiled. "Tomorrow night then?"

"Yes. And I promise that I won't forget." Leaning down, I gave him a quick peck on the lips. It wasn't a kiss of desire but something that felt habitual. Lucas looked at me with surprise in his eyes, but I quickly dressed and scampered out of the office before he could ask any questions.

The secretary gave me a knowing smile, and I flushed even more. God. Had she heard us?

"Do you need an escort out?" she asked.

"No, thanks," I muttered. "I'll be just fine."

I knew that I'd told Lucas that I was willing to explore my sexual side, but after an orgasm in his office, I was starting to wonder if I was in over my head.

THE NEXT DAY, I sat in the hard plastic seat in front of the Vice Principal's desk. I'd managed to control my frizzy curls into a hair band and wore a conservative grey skirt and jacket. I was well prepared, but that didn't stop me from feeling like a student who'd just gotten caught smoking.

"I'm sorry to keep you waiting, Ms. Whitlow," a woman said sternly as she entered the office. Torie Garret looked to be in her forties, but her hair was greying, and there were lines on her face. I would have thought running an elementary school would have been easier, but after today? After my third elementary school?

Maybe not so much. Children were terrors.

"I haven't been here long, Mrs. Garret. I'm just happy that you've found time for me. I know I'm giving you short notice."

She sat behind the desk and nodded her head. "You are late in your proposal, but you're also the first grad student we've had this year. Normally I listen to one or two proposals a semester, but Clancy Elementary is new and seems to be attractive to the university." What she didn't want to come out and say was that Clancy Elementary had been strategically zoned so that more than three-quarters of the students came from extremely wealthy families.

I didn't want to tell her that I'd just left Clancy Elementary. They'd turned me down. It wasn't that I needed wealthy kids to make my project work. In fact, the less spoiled the kids were, the better my outcome might be. Clancy just happened to be a ten minute drive from school, and Surry Elementary was thirty minutes.

But the principal had practically laughed in my face when I suggest their kids participate in summer volunteer work.

Sliding my proposal across the desk, I took a deep breath. "Middle schools and high schools offer summer school for their students. It's generally for kids to retake classes they'd failed during the regular year, but some classes are optional, and it affords a chance for students to keep their minds sharp and their hands busy during the long summer months. Elementary schools, on the other hand, don't offer anything for their students. Most parents turn to babysitters to watch their kids during the break, and there is a sprinkling of day camps in the area, but not many."

The woman looked at me sternly from over the proposal. "You want the elementary schools to offer summer programs?"

"My paper will focus on the pros and cons of such a project. I'm looking at businesses that can offer the kids some hands on experience that would be fun but still provide them some education. For the sake of my paper, I'm focusing mainly on animal rescue programs, but I'm going to hypothesize the use of nursing homes, libraries, soup kitchens, and similar charities in the area. I need sixteen students. I'm sure you know the drill. Different ages, different stages in learning, different economic backgrounds."

She put the paper down and nodded her head. "Ms. Whitlow, I think it's a wonderful idea. I've always thought the school system should be more involved in the student's life during the summer. I'm sure that you know we pull from some of the poorer families, and many of the kids are left to their own devices while the parent works. I'll go ahead and sign the paperwork for your thesis approval. Once you have everything in order, we'll send out the permission slips to the parents."

My eyes widened with excitement. "Really?"

"Ms. Whitlow, if I didn't know any better, I'd say that you were surprised," she said wryly.

Biting my lower lip, I nodded my head. "I know how late it is in the semester and how complex my program is. It's not a simple reading exercise that would only take a week or two."

"Yes, well while that might be helpful in the future, this is something that will help these kids right now. You should be very proud of yourself, Ms. Whitlow. I only hope that your program is as good as I hope."

"It will be," I promised as I stood. She scribbled her signature at the end of the paperwork and handed it back to me. "You'd better hurry if you want this in place before the summer break, Ms. Whitlow. You only have two months."

Eagerly gripping the papers to my chest, I tried to act professional, but I was practically bursting with excitement. From her smile, I knew that I wasn't fooling her, but she dismissed me with a wave of her hand. I thanked her once more before skipping from her office before she changed her mind.

Lucas Montgomery warmed my bed at night and my thesis was well on its way.

The week was getting better and better.

CHAPTER EIGHT

Sloan

W rapped in his arms, I leaned against him on the couch and snuggled. "What movie did you want to watch?" I murmured.

Lucas kissed the top of my head. "I wanted to enjoy a steak from a five-star restaurant. Staying in to order pizza and watch a movie was your idea," he reminded me.

"Five-star restaurants require makeup and dressy clothes. Randi is going to be suspicious if I keep raiding her closet, and I'm too tired to try my hand at contouring and smoky eyes."

He snorted. "I've seen you all dressed up. I doubt you spent more than five minutes on your makeup."

Lifting my head, I stared at him. "Does that bother you?"

"Why would it?"

"Reporters are always taking pictures of you. Imagine the rumors if the woman at your dinner table wasn't wearing the latest styles or newest makeup trend."

He leaned down and kissed me. Slow and easy. My toes curled, and something warm and comfortable settled in my stomach. "Sloan, I have never given a damn about the reporters. Neither should you."

Leaning over me, he grabbed the remote for the television and turned it on. "I guess you'll want to watch a romantic comedy?"

Looking horrified, I stared at him. "Are you kidding me? Your television is huge, and you have surround sound. I want to see explosions or awesome special effects."

"You are surprising," he murmured as he pulled the list of movies up. I chose one that I'd seen a hundred times. I wasn't here to see a movie or eat pizza. I was here to enjoy his company. It was amazing when his naked body was wrapped around me, but I wanted to be with him without the dirty, dirty sex.

It was dangerous. Pretending to be his girlfriend was definitely playing with fire, but he didn't seem to mind, and I was feeling daring. Things were going well.

"I haven't asked you yet. How is the search for the mole going?"

His body tensed under mind, and I wondered if that was a subject best left untouched. "Not well. There are a lot of suspects and no clear motives."

Picking up a slice of pizza, he held it up to me until I took a bite of its gooey cheesy goodness before taking a bite himself. "I can't remember the last time I had pizza."

I snorted. "Really? I have pizza at least twice a week. The pizza place is the only thing around campus open past ten. I'll probably be ten pounds fatter by the time I graduate. Would you still want me then?"

The thoughtless words were out of my mouth before I could stop them. Of course Lucas and I wouldn't still be together by the time I graduated. That would be more than six months from now. I wasn't even sure I could keep his attentions for the next two weeks.

"You'd have to eat an awful lot of pizza between now and then to gain ten pounds," he said in a neutral voice.

Diplomatic. Part of me desperately wanted to ask him how long he thought he'd be interested in me, but I knew it was dangerous territory.

"Well, I'm glad I could remind you of the common life. Tomorrow night, I'll fix you a bowl of ramen."

He wrinkled his nose, and I laughed. "No? How about grilled cheese?"

"I offer to take you to the nicest restaurants, and you offer to make me ramen and grilled cheese. How is that fair?"

I stole another bite of his pizza and smiled. "I had no idea that our agreement was based on fairness."

He stared at me and ran his hands down my body. Even though there was lust in his eyes, I could have sworn there was something else. "No, it's not." His voice was husky when he leaned down and kissed me. Setting the slice down on the plate, he moved his hand up under my shirt, and soon the movie and the pizza were forgotten.

RANDI WAS WAITING for me when I snuck back into the apartment just after dawn. I would have left for class directly from the Montgomery estates, but I'd forgotten my books. Lucas was up before the sun and doing push-ups in the bedroom.

Otherwise, I would have been back sooner, but there was something incredibly sexy about watching him exercise naked.

I was impressed with how many sit-ups he could do while I was straddling him.

"I got in an hour ago," Randi accused. "Imagine my surprise when your bed was still made. I know damn well that you were not at the library, so you might as well tell me the truth."

I could still smell Lucas on me. "I thought you'd be happy that I was having some fun."

"Of course I am. I'm worried that you're not telling me about it. Sloan, be honest with me. Are you still sleeping with Montgomery?"

She crossed her arms and stared at me. Taking a deep breath, I let the bag slip from my shoulders. "Would it really be so bad if I was?"

"If it was anyone but you, I would say no. Sloan, he's going to hurt you."

Jutting my chin out defiantly, I glared at her. "Randi, I'm an adult. I can make my own decisions. Lucas and I have an agreement that's purely sexual. It's been a great way for me to release my tension. I think I'm quite good at this casual sex thing."

"And what's his interest in you?" She immediately closed her eyes and shook her head. "Shit, Sloan. I didn't mean it like that."

"I know exactly what you meant," I growled as I grabbed my bag. "You think I'm not pretty enough or exotic enough to catch the attention of Lucas. Why don't you just admit it? Are you jealous?"

"Sloan, you know damn well that's not what's going on here. Yes, Lucas can have his pick of women. He likes them powerful. He's just playing with you, Sloan. As much as you might hate to admit it, you're not the kind of woman who fucks a man at night and forgets them the next morning. He's not the man who settles down with someone. You know that I'm right, but you're ignoring it. If you get lost in whatever fantasy keeps playing in your head, you're going to get hurt."

I felt nothing but cold anger as I stared at her. God, I knew she was right, but this was something I had to prove to myself. "That's my problem and not yours. Next time, mind your own damn business."

She gasped, but I was already halfway to my room. Slamming the door shut, I leaned against it and tried not to cry. Deep down, I did want her to find out. I wanted someone to talk to, but it was obvious that Randi was not going to support me.

We'd never fought. At least not like that. We'd argued over music and noise levels. I sometimes lost my patience with her when she forgot to clean the dishes, and she'd snap at me when I forgot the groceries. But this was different.

This had actually hurt.

The shower started, and I knew that I wasn't going to get the chance to bathe before class. The scent of Lucas and sex would follow me around all day.

I wasn't exactly upset about that.

Stuffing the books in my bag, I tried to put the argument behind me as I grabbed a blueberry muffin from the kitchen and shoved it in my mouth. Opening the door, I walked straight into Matthew.

Matthew Rehn was my odd neighbor. He was handsome, but he worked odd hours and never spoke much. Randi and I had talked endlessly about our theories about him.

At best, he was a secret CIA agent. At worse, he was a serial killer.

But he was always nice to us, so we didn't bother him much. I couldn't hide the surprise from my face when I saw him.

"Matthew!"

The muffin was still in my mouth and muffled the sound. He lifted an eyebrow and smiled at me. "I've caught you at a bad time."

Pulling the muffin out of my mouth, I swallowed. "I'm sorry. I do know not to talk with my mouth full. I was just on my way to school."

"Right." He handed me an envelope. "This was at my door last night. I tried to deliver it then, but neither you or your roommate were home. It's addressed to you, but there's no postage on it. Were you expecting something?"

I shoved the muffin back in my mouth and shook my head as I took the envelope. I could have put down my keys, but that didn't occur to me until after I looked like a complete idiot in front of my neighbor.

"Right," he laughed softly. "Have a good day."

I stole a peak around the doorway as I watched him enter his own apartment. One of these days I was going to figure him out.

Shoving the envelope under my arm, I locked the door behind me and shuffled to the car. After only a couple of hours of sleep, I desperately needed coffee.

Although it made me late, once again, to Dr. Elliot's class, I did stop for coffee. Luckily, my professor didn't interrupt class this time to berate me.

After the lecture, I pulled the signed form for my thesis experiment from my bag and hurried down the steps. "Dr. Elliot?"

"Is your alarm clock still broken, Ms. Whitlow?" he said without looking up.

Damn. He did notice. "No. I just didn't get much sleep last night," I muttered.

"I assume that's because you were working on your thesis?"

Only if my thesis included a gorgeous naked man on the couch. And the bed. And the floor. "I got permission from Surry Elementary school. I'm in the middle of speaking with Lab Rescue and High Tails Humane Society. They're both looking over the information, but I think High Tails has already decided to work with me. They have until Monday to get back to me, and then hopefully I can start drawing up an itinerary."

"Excellent. Keep pushing the way you are, and I know you'll be ready for this summer. It will have to be a full twelve-week program. You won't be able to cut it short in order to have more time for your analysis."

"I know. I'm not going to take any short-cuts."

"Good." He finally turned to eye me. "Ms. Whitlow, I'm sure you're aware that Montgomery Industries is a big supporter of the school."

"What?" Surprised, I stared at him. "I didn't know that. Why are you telling me this?"

He looked like he wanted to say something before he shook his head. "It's not important. I'm sure you're acting ethically and morally in your actions."

Shoulders slumping, I stared at him. He knew. He knew that I was sleeping with Lucas, and he thought I was using that power to push my thesis along.

But how did he know?

More importantly, why did he think I was the kind of woman who would use sex to my advantage?

"You have nothing to worry about," I said softly as I lowered my gaze. "I've worked hard to get where I am now, and there is nothing but hard work driving me."

"Of course. I don't mean to imply otherwise."

But he did, and we both knew it.

"Have a good weekend, professor."

"Email me if you need me for anything," he said absently, but he didn't look me in the eye.

For some reason, I couldn't meet his eye either. I had nothing to feel guilty about, but that didn't stop the knot from forming in my stomach.

Is that what everyone would think?

It wasn't until I got back to the car that I remembered the envelope. Sitting in the stuffy heat, I pulled it out and ripped it open.

Nothing could have prepared me for what I found. Pictures. One right after the other.

All of them with Lucas and Iris. Naked and in different stages of ecstasy.

"It's in the past," I whispered. "It has nothing to do with me."

My hands shook as I shuffled through them. Even though I knew what it would do to me, I couldn't stop.

There was a note at the end.

This is who he is with during every lunch break. You seem like a nice girl. I thought you should know.

CHAPTER NINE

Lucas

"The expansion into Japan is going well. The factory should be up and running sometime next month," I said tonelessly as I tried not to yawn. It wasn't just that I didn't get much sleep last night. There were easy moments with Sloan. Time where it felt comfortable and natural. But when she was in my bed, I gave her everything I had. I was driven by every moan, every quiver, every soft sound that I could wrench from her pretty little mouth.

It was perfect and exhausting.

"And Boston?" Jenson asked hotly. "We're not here to talk about Japan. I want to know why you've halted the search for real estate in Boston. We projected next quarter using those numbers."

Just two years ago, Jenson was nothing more than the irresponsible son of an extremely wealthy family. His mother was born into old money, and his father owned a pharmaceutical company. His mother died years ago of cancer, and he lost his father in a house fire. Jenson had immediately sold the company and had millions to play with.

He had a hand in several pies around the country, but he seemed to enjoy investing in me. I wanted to smack the smile right off the little asshole's face, but his father and my father had been good friends. If he were older, we might have grown up friends.

I couldn't fault him. He was just bringing up what everyone was thinking. I had to handle this carefully.

"I was given some new information last week, and it has caused me to reconsider the Boston project."

Jenson smirked. "And what was that?"

"Some information that could greatly affect the Boston economy. That should play out over the next month, and then I'll decide whether or not we should make the move or not."

Addison cleared her throat. "What information would that be? Who is your source?"

I smiled. "Mrs. Addison, I have always shared pertinent information with the members of the board. I only withhold now because if you knew, you could be a witness against me."

There was nervous laughter in the room, and I knew I'd covered the issue for now. We concluded the meeting, and when it was just myself and Hamburg left, Torrence joined us.

"Did you see anything suspicious?" I asked in a low voice.

Torrence shook his head. "Nothing. If it's a board member, they've covering their tracks. You handled the situation well."

"That's true," Hamburg grunted. "Meeting was a damn waste of time. You didn't tell us anything new."

"That's the point," I said softly. "I hate to distrust my own board, but I can't risk any sensitive information getting out."

As soon as the words were out of my mouth, Torrence's phone rang. I saw the tension in his mouth when he looked at the screen.

"Who is it?" I asked in a low voice.

He didn't answer. Turning his back to me, he held the phone up to his ear. His shoulder's tightened in anger, but he only thanked the caller and hung up.

"Torrence, what the hell is going on?" I demanded.

"There was a press release in the DC newspaper," he said softly. "Something about a merger with Garland Software."

I froze and stared at him. "That's not possible," I muttered in a low voice.

"Montgomery?" Hamburg growled. "What is he talking about? We've never discussed a merger."

A shudder crawled down my spine. "That's because the information never left my office. My private office. In my house."

"God," Torrence muttered. "You've got to be kidding me."

"David Garland contacted me three weeks ago. He wants to retire, but he's afraid his son will run the business into the ground. He wants to sell it to me so long as it could keep his name. I told him that I would think about it, but we both knew that I would agree. It's a lucrative buy. The conversation never left the office. It never made it past the fucking phone. Torrence, you swept my home. You didn't find anything."

"No," he said quietly. "So someone placed the bug and removed it without you knowing. They had access to your home, Montgomery. That's incredibly dangerous."

He didn't have to tell me twice. My mind was already whirling as I tried to think of the people who had been in and out of the house. I had a cleaning staff. People to maintain the grounds and the pool. The cleaning staff had a key, but they were thoroughly investigated. They were also the only ones allowed in my house without supervision.

"Torrence," I said softly.

"I'll look into your staff. You still have your security cameras up and working?" he asked gravely.

I nodded. "I'll stop by tonight and have a look at the monitors. Please let me send someone home with you until I can get there."

"No. If I do anything out of the ordinary, they'll know. Come when you can."

"Lucas."

"I can take care of myself."

"What about the company that you keep," he reminded me softly.

Sloan. "That's a low blow, Drew." But he wasn't wrong. Sloan had spent the night with me. I'd licked every inch of her naked body, and for all I know, someone could have been listening.

It made my blood boil.

"It won't be a problem. She won't be setting foot anywhere near the estates." I would not put her in danger. No matter how badly I wanted her. "Hamburg, you don't breathe a word of this to anyone. I'll speak to Garland myself and see what he wants to do next. His stocks are probably going through the roof."

The older man watched me carefully. "You can't keep this a secret for long. The board is going to know about the leak. DC isn't some small town. News of the merger will reach them."

"Nothing has been finalized. I'll contact the newspaper and let them know they've made an error. Pressure them to retract the article. If the board asks, we can blame the leak on Garland."

"Fine," he muttered. I stared at him. Was it my imagination, or was he in a hurry to make sure news of the mole went public? He'd brought the first leak to my attention, but that didn't mean that he wasn't involved.

"Torrence, do whatever you need to do here. Send someone to campus to keep an eye on Sloan. She'll probably be at the library until they close. I do not want her to know what's going on."

"How many times do I have to call you an idiot before you realize that I'm right?" he rolled his eyes but left the office.

Hamburg faced me, and I saw the troubled look in his eyes. "Montgomery, I'm afraid this is getting personal. We should call the police."

"I can take care of this on my own."

"You are your father's son. It's going to get you in serious trouble one day," he said with a sigh.

I was my father's son. And it made me millions. I wouldn't let anything slow me down now.

I walked through the house slowly and wondered why the hell I stayed here. I barely used a quarter of the rooms. Most of the house only saw the footsteps of my cleaning staff.

It had never really felt like home. Even when I was a kid, it didn't feel like home. My father was meticulous about what could and couldn't be touched. I'd spent most of the time in my room, and even though I was master and sleeping in the biggest room of the estate, some things hadn't changed.

The night lounging with Sloan on the couch was the most fun I'd had in the house in years.

Now that I knew someone had violated the house, it felt like mine. My home. My domain. My personal space.

Cold anger fueled me, but nothing looked out of place. I moved quietly from room to room and it wasn't until the doorbell sounded that I finally stopped.

Opening the door, I glared at the gorgeous blonde. Iris. "What the hell are you doing here?" I snapped. "I thought I made it clear that I didn't want to see you anymore."

She just gave me a smug smile and pushed past me. "Calm down, darling. I'm just here to talk. The least you can do is offer a girl a drink."

I didn't budge. "What do you want to talk about?"

She ignored me and walked through the foyer. With a

sinking feeling, I closed the door and followed her. "Iris," I said in a warning voice.

"You always did have the best scotch," she said as she pulled open the wet bar in my living room. "I didn't hear the rumors until I got back to the states. The rumors that you were monogamous. It wasn't until I saw you with her that I believed them. She's such a mousy little thing. Easy for you to control? I bet she's a submissive bitch in bed." Her eyes glazed over. "Oh, we could have so much fun with her."

"Enough."

The anger in my voice snapped her back to attention. "My, my," she purred. "You don't actually have feelings for her, do you?"

"My feelings are none of your business, Iris. We had a couple good months together, but we both knew it wouldn't be more than that. You left to do God knows what in Europe, and that should have been the end of it."

She tossed the scotch back and bent over as she searched the bottles on the bottom. I knew the move was deliberate. Her short skirt rose high enough until I could clearly see that she wore nothing underneath. "If you're here to seduce me, you're wasting your time." There was a time when I would have eagerly sunk into her, but she just didn't do it for me anymore.

She straightened and smiled. "I'd be lying if I didn't say that I was hoping to have a little fun today. I have some information, and I thought that maybe you could pay me for it. The way you used to pay me."

"I don't require your information anymore, Iris."

"Really? So you've successfully ferreted out that mole yourself?"

That got my attention. I watched her as she sat on the couch and patted the seat next to her. "Come on, baby. I know you want to."

I didn't move from the doorframe. "I do want your information, but I'm not about to fuck you for it. If you want money —"

She waved her hand dismissively. "I have plenty of money," Iris said with a pout. "What I really want is to feel that cock in my mouth again."

"Not going to happen. Get out."

Sighing, she rolled her eyes and leaned back. "Fine. But I'm a good person. I'll still give you the information."

A few second passed. "I'm waiting."

"Really? You can't even sit next to me?"

Knowing damn well that it was a bad idea, I crossed the room and sat on the other end of the couch. I'd get the information and haul her ass out of my house. If there was one thing Iris was very good at, it was discovering people's dark secrets. If she had information, it would probably be good.

I heard the front door open and turned my head. "Hang on," I muttered as I moved to push myself up.

Before I could even blink, Iris straddled me and pushed me into the couch.

"Iris? What the fuck," I muttered as I grabbed her hips.

She slid her damp pussy over my and moaned just as I saw the figure walk through the door.

"Oh my God." Sloan stared at me, her eyes full of pain. Papers fell from her fingers and fluttered to the ground. "I am such an idiot."

"Goddammit, Sloan, wait," I shouted as I threw Iris off me and stood. Iris yelled in indignation as she hit the floor, but I didn't care. I ran for Sloan, but she was already down the hall and out the door.

"Sloan!" Bursting out of the house, I watched helplessly as she made a beeline for her car.

"Don't," she shouted as she turned. "Just don't come near me. I don't do this. I'm not this woman that just sleeps with a man, but I gave you everything that you wanted. I asked you for one thing, Lucas. Just one, and you couldn't do it."

"Sloan," I growled as I started towards her, but she was already slipping in her car and starting it. By the time I reached her, she was pealing down the driveway.

As she drove away, I saw that she never even looked back.

Two minutes. It couldn't have been any longer than that. Two minutes from the time that she'd walked into the house and driven like a bat out of hell out of my life.

CHAPTER TEN

Lucas

"It's okay, baby," Iris whispered. She ran her hands over my shoulders, and I quickly shrugged her off. I couldn't even turn around to look at her.

"You have thirty seconds to get the fuck off my property. If you come anywhere near me or Sloan, you will not like the consequences."

"Lucas! What the hell has gotten into you? She's nobody!"

"And yet I would still choose her over you. Any time. Every time."

"If you deny me now, I will never tell you what I know. This isn't some pissed off employee that you're facing, Lucas. This person is out for blood, and they aren't going to stop until they have it."

I felt numb. When her words finally penetrated me, I turned and stared at her. A smiled spread over her face when she thought that maybe I would give her what she wanted. "I would rather lose everything than give you anything that you want. Get. Out. Now."

I'd never seen Iris look uncertain, but her mouth opened

slightly and her eyes widened. For a second, I thought she was going to argue, but she turned and ran from the house. I didn't even bother to watch her get into her car. My only concern was Sloan.

Bolting for the house, I quickly snagged my phone and called her. It went straight to voicemail. "Sloan, I need to explain. Call me."

To be on the safe side, I texted her as well.

It's not what you think. Call me. Text me. Now.

No one denied me. Until now. I waited all night, but she didn't call me back.

First there was anger. She should have damn well trusted me. She should have at least stuck around so I could explain.

I started on the bottle of scotch. Someone sent those pictures. Iris? She wouldn't have dared. Iris was calculating and cruel, but she wasn't an idiot. She would never have done something that could have easily been traced back to her.

The mole. Iris was right. They weren't just trying to destroy my reputation. They were out to ruin me.

I DIDN'T KNOW why I came back here. Club 9 was packed with bodies. I didn't even bother to make my way to the second floor where I could have had more privacy. I lifted the glass of whiskey to my lips and downed it.

It was my fifth one of the night. My eyes moved over the people undulating on the floor, grinding their bodies on each other. They were so starved for attention. Many of them would go home with a stranger in hopes the lackluster sex would give them a little relief from the loneliness.

I hadn't seen Sloan in a week. I desperately wanted to explain what she had seen. I wanted to explain that the photos in her hands were before I even met her. I wanted to make it right. Even if she didn't come back to me, I needed her to at least not hate me.

Randi just coldly informed me that Sloan was working on her thesis some place private. I tried to get Torrence to search for her, but he'd told me to let it go.

I nearly fired him over it.

The week had felt like months in hell.

And now it was over. It was probably for the best. I could focus on work.

I could fuck whomever I wanted.

As I signaled to the bartender that I wanted another drink, a tight body in a slinky red dress squeezed herself next to me. "Hi," she said in a sultry voice.

Deliberately, I cocked my head as my eyes roamed down her body. Nice perky tits. A full round ass. Cock-sucking cherry-red lipstick. Lustful eyes that told me everything I wanted to know.

She'd let me take her home and do whatever I wanted.

"Hi," I muttered.

"Buy a girl a drink?"

"Do you really need a drink?"

Her eyes widened in surprise before she laughed. "No one has ever asked me that before. You look like the kind of man I could spend a little time with completely sober."

"I'm not a happy man right now," I said softly.

"I don't need you to be happy. I just need you to be hard."

It wasn't enough to make me stir, but it was enough to grab my attention. The next glass of whiskey appeared in front of me, and I knocked it back while she watched. I didn't say anything as I sat it on the counter.

"So what do you say? Take a girl some place more private?"

What did I say to that?

The best way to get over one woman was with another. I had

done nothing wrong to Sloan. There was no reason I couldn't enjoy the sexy and willing woman in front of me.

Signaling to the bartender, I pointed to my empty glass and held up two fingers.

"Does that mean you're going to buy me a drink after all?" she said as she put a hand on my chest.

"Nothing wrong with buying a gorgeous woman a drink," I muttered.

Nothing wrong with that at all.

BOOK THREE: WHEN HE LOVES

REVENGE. LUST. RESOLVE

Lucas had been on his way to putting the feisty, redhead, Sloan, behind him forever when she showed back up. Just as he was set to forget her, watching her without her knowing, ignited the fire which had been slumbering inside of him for her.

SLOAN FOUND herself face to face with the man who she thought had betrayed her trust. She wasn't pleased to see another woman on his arm again. A thing Lucas made sure she saw.

SLOAN RAN from the scene and as she fled the club, she saw a couple of interesting people in the parking lot who didn't even notice her as she'd donned a jet black wig for the evening.

NOW THAT SHE was fairly certain who was setting Lucas up, she felt compelled to let him in on what she saw. As she sat in her car, she waited and watched and learned a hell of a lot.

. . .

SHE'D GOTTEN RID OF LUCAS' phone number so she wouldn't be tempted to call him and she'd blocked his number so there was no way to reach him. She'd have to go see him to tell him and she knew that it would be hard to stay in control of her body that ached for the man.

BUT WHEN SHE WAS SPOTTED, the chase began and the odds were against her as she tried to get to Lucas before they got to her.

Get ready for more twists and turns as Lucas and Sloan reach the conclusion of their arrangement, forever.

CHAPTER ONE

Sloan

Randi put the finishing touches on my made up face and made sure the jet black wig of long, straight hair was securely fastened to my head as I slipped into the tall heels she let me borrow. She didn't have to push me too hard to make me go out with her. I needed a distraction, a huge distraction to help me put Lucas out of my mind.

Thank God for my thesis work or I'd never have had the self-control to stay away from him. I don't know why I ever let myself believe in the man. He was a playboy, plain and simple. No matter how it had felt, it was as fake as he was.

At least now I knew that for certain.

I'd let Randi glob on the makeup and put the wig on me as well as one of her tight dresses to make myself look completely different. Not that I was trying to hide, but I was trying to be someone else for the night.

My plan was to let my inhibitions go, for that night, anyway. My sexual sessions with Lucas had loosened me up. I felt sexier than ever as I now had knowledge that I wasn't a drag in bed and Lucas taught me a lot too. So I was looking for a piece of strange man to make me feel better.

I didn't care about much, I just wanted a man to make me feel like I wasn't the biggest damn idiot in the world. I wanted to know if I really was attractive to the opposite sex or did Lucas pick me because he knew I was neither sexy nor smart enough to find out he was fucking someone else on his lunch hour.

And that total rich bitch at that!

The only thing I feel bad about is not slapping the shit out of them both. Now that would've felt great and maybe then I'd have some closure. But I felt like there were some strings left untied. Some things I'd like to have known but knew I never would because I couldn't ever talk to that man again. I deleted his phone number and blocked his phone numbers so he couldn't call me. I thought of it all and went away this last week to stay with another friend of mine because I knew he'd come to my apartment to try to get his, dumb ass, piece of ass, back.

But I'd grown smarter and would not be slipping back into that man's bed, no matter how nice it felt. I actually thought we were getting close!

We'd sit on the couch watching television and doing lame shit that couples do. We'd play footsie under the sheets each morning then have awesome morning sex and I could swear he looked at me with my bedhead and sleep filled eyes with something more than lust and desire. I could swear I saw caring and even a touch of love in his dark eyes.

I shook my head to clear it, I needed to stop thinking about that asshole!

"Time to go!" Randi shouted as she clapped her hands, enthusiastically. "I can't believe I talked you into this!"

"I have to get out." I got up and grabbed my purse and put

the long strap over my shoulder and around my neck to make sure it stayed securely with me. I planned on shaking my booty that night, come hell or high water, I was going to have fun if it killed me!

As we walked out to the parking lot, Randi took my hand and started dragging me to her car. "You're coming with me."

"No!" I shouted as I pulled out of her grasp. "Randi, I'm taking my car tonight. I have to be able to escape if I start to have a meltdown. Or I may need it to take my ass to some guy's place and I'll need to have a ride home."

"I get you," she winked at me. "Okay, take your car and I'll take mine. But stay close so we can walk into the club together. If I go in alone, I'll get scooped up and we won't even get to have one drink together before the mating rituals kick in."

We high-fived and walked away to our separate cars. I was a little worried about what she'd say about me taking my own car and I was happy she didn't try to change my mind.

I followed her to the Club 9, the place where it all started, and we parked next to each other. As we walked in, side by side, I could've sworn I heard a familiar man's voice and the giggle of some woman. But when I turned to look back, I saw no one.

I had hoped it was not the beginning of a paranoid night. If I kept hearing men who were close to Lucas, I wasn't going to have a very good time.

Randi took us straight to the bar with the good looking bartender who eyed me for a moment then he laughed and pointed at me with a big grin on his pretty handsome face. "You! The redhead, right?"

I was flattered that he remembered me. That had been weeks ago and yet he even recognized me under all the makeup and the wig. "Wow! How did you remember me?"

He leaned in close as he set two tequila shots on the bar in front of him. "Your eyes, sweetheart. And these are on the house.

You and your friend are on me tonight. Just remember to come back to my bar for all of them, I'd like to see a hell of a lot more of you. I'm Clark, by the way. And you are?"

Wow, already, a hit! "My names, Sloan." I stuck my hand out to shake his and he took it with a laugh and shook it. "Nice to meet you, Clark."

He looked to one side and gave the other guy working with him a nod. "Cover for me, will you, Steve? I'd like to take this fine young thing out on the dance floor for her first dance of the night."

I was shocked. I hadn't even been there but two minutes and already I had a very hot prospect. Before I knew it, I was gathered up by the man and taken out to the dance floor where he held me tight while we gravitated our bodies to the hard beat.

Thanks to Lucas, I had learned how to really shake my hips and move my body in ways that seemed to entice the man. Clark was pretty built himself, his eyes were a light green and he had a happy go lucky demeanor. Nothing like Lucas.

I found myself comparing them as his cock pressed up against me as we seemingly dry humped each other on the dance floor. Everyone else was dancing like that, so why not?

But something was missing. I felt no heat. No urgency to fuck him. He was handsome and had a dimple in one of his cheeks. He dressed nice, smelled great, I mean there was not one thing wrong with him except for the fact he was not Lucas.

So I decided I'd just have to drink until I forgot about Lucas and could only see Clark in my future. My future for that night, anyway. We danced for a little while longer then I saw him look around me at the line at the bar and he let out a deep sigh. "Sadly, I have to end this. I have work to do. Come sit at the bar and I'll fill you full of alcohol and dance with you again as soon as I clear up that line."

I gave him a nod and he took my hand and led me back to

the bar. But just before he let my hand go to go back behind the bar, He pulled me in very fast and kissed me hard.

Our tongues roamed around the others and I could hear some cheering from the people waiting to get something to drink. Then he pulled back and held our clasped hands up. "She's with me, tonight, boys! So hands off!"

Then he took me to a barstool close to where he'd be working and I felt happy. So damn happy that I really was attractive enough for that man to remember me and be so possessive of me from the get go. Then my happiness turned into aggravation.

What was I doing? Was I really about to let myself become another man's possession? Why in the world did every man I met suddenly want me for themselves? And was that a really such a bad thing?"

I was about to be twenty-five. The age when a lot of women get into serious relationships. Those kind of relationships that move into marriage and family. I was of the age to become someone's everything. And the guy behind the bar was giving me all the right signals that he'd very much like that.

He placed a very nice looking drink in front of me before he took a single order and leaned over and gave me a quick kiss before he got busy taking care of the other people. Some woman leaned in to say, "He must really love you. How long have you two been together?"

"We aren't," I told her.

She fanned herself and said, "Well, get ready for some action tonight. That man has a definite hard on for just you."

I looked back to find Clark pouring and shaking drinks and the moment I looked back, he caught me looking and gave me a smile. "Having fun?"

I nodded and sipped my drink that tasted like a strawberry

vanilla milkshake. It was yummy and creamy and nothing like a drink Lucas would've ordered for me. Then I turned to look out at the people dancing on the dancefloor and thought I saw, Lucas.

Why can't I get him out of my mind?

CHAPTER TWO

Lucas

I hadn't seen Sloan in a week. I desperately wanted to explain what she had seen. I wanted to explain that the photos in her hands were before I even met her. I wanted to make it right. Even if she didn't come back to me, I needed her to at least not hate me.

Randi just coldly informed me that Sloan was working on her thesis some place private. I tried to get Torrence to search for her, but he'd told me to let it go.

I nearly fired him over it.

The week had felt like months in hell.

And now it was over. It was probably for the best. I could focus on work.

I could fuck whomever I wanted.

As I signaled to the bartender that I wanted another drink, a tight body in a slinky red dress squeezed herself next to me. "Hi," she said in a sultry voice.

Deliberately, I cocked my head as my eyes roamed down her body. Nice perky tits. A full round ass. Cock-sucking cherry-red lipstick. Lustful eyes that told me everything I wanted to know.

She'd let me take her home and do whatever I wanted.

"Hi," I muttered.

"Buy a girl a drink?"

"Do you really need a drink?"

Her eyes widened in surprise before she laughed. "No one has ever asked me that before. You look like the kind of man I could spend a little time with completely sober."

"I'm not a happy man right now," I said softly.

"I don't need you to be happy. I just need you to be hard."

It wasn't enough to make me stir, but it was enough to grab my attention. The next glass of whiskey appeared in front of me, and I knocked it back while she watched. I didn't say anything as I sat it on the counter.

"So what do you say? Take a girl some place more private?"

What did I say to that?

The best way to get over one woman was with another. I had done nothing wrong to Sloan. There was no reason I couldn't enjoy the sexy and willing woman in front of me.

Signaling to the bartender, I pointed to my empty glass and held up two fingers.

"Does that mean you're going to buy me a drink after all?" she said as she put a hand on my chest.

"Nothing wrong with buying a gorgeous woman a drink," I muttered.

Nothing wrong with that at all.

Only, something inside me told it was wrong. Something in my head told me to get up and walk away from the vixen. But then the drinks came and I took mine and took a drink and looked her over again. I could've used a good roll in the sheets. God knows I missed sex. But the sex I missed was with Sloan and that wasn't going to happen again.

I wasn't even sure if she showed back up and told me she was sorry for not trusting me and not giving me a chance to explain things to her, it would be enough for me to take her back. To tell her we could go back to our agreement and continue as if she never went off the deep end.

"My name is, Veronica," the woman said. Her blonde hair was pulled back into a clip and she let it out of the clip, making it fall around her narrow shoulders. "And you are Lucas Montgomery."

"I am," I said as I looked into her light blue eyes that were almost gray and found no depth to them at all. So I said something to see if she had any. "How'd you like to get fucked by the Lucas Montgomery?" I took another drink and watched her eyes light up.

Her hand moved over my shoulder and she leaned in. "I'd do anything for you. And I do mean anything."

Her breath was warm on my face and the smell of the liquor was unappealing. The way her hand moved over my thigh and up to touch my cock, which wasn't at all enthused with her, made my skin kind of crawl. But she was a warm body that had the parts necessary to please me for a little while so what the hell.

Then my mind slipped in a word that came out of my mouth without me realizing it, "Why?"

She blinked and pulled her head back and looked at me with a confused expression. "What do you mean?"

I shook my head to rid myself of the depth Sloan had brought into my life. Sloan would never say anything so stupid and simple before really knowing a man.

But I needed to stop comparing women to Sloan or I'd never want to fuck another one again. So I ran my hand along her jaw and whispered, "I want to take you in my car first and if you please me, then I'll take you to my place. But I have to warn you,

I'm not a happy man at this time and I feel the need to take out some aggressions. You don't mind a spanking, do you?"

Her face came close to mine and her lips brushed mine as she spoke, "Not from you, I don't. Tie me up and do with me what you want, Mr. Montgomery. I am yours for the taking."

As hard as she was trying and as much as she was willing to give to me, it wasn't enough. "Let me think on it, Veronica."

She sat back and took a drink from the short glass and when she did I could see down out of the second story to the dance-floor on the ground floor. And there was a woman dancing with some man and making movements that caught my eye.

The way she was all up on him had me hot in a flash. I stood up and walked out to look at them over the balcony. Her dress was tight and red. Her hair was black but it was obviously a wig, a cheap one at that. I looked all the way down to her shoes and they were black and shiny.

There was something about the woman, the way she moved, and the way her curves filled that dress out. Then they moved around a little and I saw her face.

"Sloan!"

She had a ton of makeup on and that damn wig to cover her wild red hair, but it was her. That alabaster skin and those emerald eyes told me as much. When you threw in the way she was moving her body, I had no doubt.

Suddenly the man was saying something to her and he led her off the dancefloor. I watched every step they took and when they got to the bar he pulled her in and kissed her.

I stopped breathing, stopped thinking, and had to stop myself from hauling ass down to get her. I watched her hands move up and hold his shoulders as they obviously kissed using tongues and my insides turned to acid.

How could she?

Then they stopped kissing and he held up their hands and

said something that had the people around them cheering and I watched him pick her up and set her down on a barstool then he went behind it and she was smiling like she was the happiest girl in the world.

My heart was barely beating. She was truly done with me. She must've moved on to that guy soon after that day she threw the pictures on the floor and left me.

I guess the looks I had been seeing in her eyes were all lies. I thought I saw more there as we spent our evenings and nights together. I thought I saw caring and even a little love in her big green eyes. But it couldn't have been if she moved on so damn quickly.

Fuck! It's only been a week!

Soft hands moved over my arms as I'd rolled up my sleeves. A soft voice whispered to me, "I'm ready to go when you are."

Veronica was right behind me. All ready for me. So I placed my drink on the little table next to the railing and turned back to her. "After a dance."

Nearly dragging her down the stairs, I made my way to the dancefloor and made sure I got close enough so I could easily drift us close enough for Sloan to see me from her perch on the barstool her new lover had placed her on.

I caught them kissing again as he placed some drink in front of her and fury nearly consumed me. How could she move on so quickly?

I knew we had this agreement to just have sex and keep it light but damn it! She wouldn't even give me a chance to explain that Iris was being a slut like always and I was throwing her out. I wasn't even going to get any information out of her. And I desperately needed that information.

During the last week, not one bit of information had come up to get us any closer to finding out who the hell was out to ruin me. And I sure could've used Sloan at my side. I needed her like I had never needed anyone. And she just left!

I danced us over and when we got close enough, I moved in and took Veronica by the waist and pulled her into me as I ground on her and kept heading toward Sloan who was chatting it up with some woman.

When the woman stepped back in line to order a drink, I saw Sloan's eyes roam over the dancing crowd and made sure I was turned toward her. I was not far from her at all and stared right at her as her eyes moved over me then right back to me.

Her mouth fell open and she looked shocked. Then she was up and hauling ass. I took Veronica's hand and pulled her along with me as I easily caught up to Sloan and grabbed her by the shoulder.

As she spun around, I threw my arm around the little blonde and found myself saying, "What's up?"

"Fuck you, Lucas!" she shouted as she eyed the woman under my arm. "I see you've found yourself another fuck buddy, congratulations!"

Then something came out of Veronica's mouth that might have really fucked things up. "Yes, he has, he eats pussy like no man I've ever met. Shame you left him. But good for me. I sit on his fat cock six or seven times a day. He tells me I'm a thousand times better than you, bitch!"

Sloan's eyes went huge then she reached out and slapped the shit out of me. I was stunned long enough for her to get lost in the crowd and escape from me. I looked at the girl under my arm and pulled it off of her quickly. "Are you insane?"

She grabbed my hand. "Let her go. I want you, Lucas. She clearly doesn't. Come on, let's go to your car like you promised."

I couldn't find Sloan at all then I felt a hand on my shoulder. "Hey, mister, excuse me please," the fucking guy she was dancing with said as he moved past me, obviously trying to get to Sloan.

He sure did have his eyes on her and that made me furious. So I went after him with Veronica hanging onto me, trying desperately to hold me back as she screeched something about not needing the bitch.

But all I could think about is how much I did need her. All I could see was red when I kept picturing her kissing that man who was merely steps ahead of me. The something slammed into the side of my head and I was down.

CHAPTER THREE

Sloan

My heart was pounding as I went as fast as I could in the sky high heels to get the hell away from Lucas and that slut with the tight-ass dress and fake tits. Just as I reached the door, I heard a man calling my name and it wasn't Lucas' deep voice. I turned back and caught a glimpse of Clark coming after me and looked at the bouncer who was between me and the exit.

"Can you tell him that I'm really sorry but I have to get the fuck out of here?" I asked the very large man who was looking at me with a frown.

He stepped aside and said, "I'll tell him."

As I stepped out the door, I reached down and took my heels off and ran straight for my car. It was parked behind several others so I was pretty sure Lucas wouldn't see it from the door. If he went so far as to actually search the parking lot, he'd find me, but I highly doubted he'd be doing that now that he had that tramp to suck his cock.

I slipped behind the steering wheel and laid the seat back to make sure no one could see me. If I turned the car on and tried to speed away, he might chase me and then I'd be trapped for sure and have to talk to him.

The night was a little on the hot and humid side so I cracked both the driver's and passenger's windows as I waited for the right time to leave.

As I was hunched down, waiting, a voice drifted through the parking lot, it was quiet and feminine and I recognized it but couldn't quite put my finger on who it was.

"She should be coming out with him any minute, her text said she had him in her clutches," the female voice said.

I heard a smacking sound that kind of sounded like a messy kiss then I heard a man say, "He's about to meet the end of his rule as Washington's wealthiest man. It's time for our benefactor to get the justice she requires."

"Lucas sure fucked up when he hurt that lady," the woman said.

My ears perked up and I found myself listening even harder when I heard his name. Who had he hurt and was that the person who was out to ruin him?

The man made a deep chuckle and with that little laugh I recognized him, "Drew Torrence, the head of his security team!" I whispered.

My windows were tinted in the back more so than in the front so I slipped between the seats and made my way to the back so I could try to see where they were and try to get a picture with my cell phone if possible. Now I knew why Torrence wanted to do things himself and leave the cops out of everything!

As I looked around, I finally found the car where the voices were coming from. It wasn't the car Torrence usually drove. It was a small, blue car with darkly tinted windows. But the windows were all about a third of the way down and I could clearly see the man in the driver's seat.

Torrence moved a little to reposition himself as he said, "Lila Sheffield was definitely not a woman he should've loved and left. She's dead-set on making him pay for not finding her more to his satisfaction."

The woman leaned forward and I saw her too. It was his secretary, Cecelia. I nearly shouted when I saw her. Lucas trusted that woman with everything. How could she do this to him?

And who was Lila Sheffield?

Taking my phone out of my little purse, I Googled her name and immediately found out who she was. A very wealthy woman in her own right as she was the owner of several large companies in the New York area.

She looked a lot like that Iris bitch and as I read through things more, I found a little bit of interesting information. Iris was the other woman's cousin it seemed. So now the sudden appearance of the other woman made perfect sense. Iris was part of this thing too!

It seemed there were quite a few people who wanted to bring Lucas Montgomery down and I mean all the way down. So far down that he had to lose me too.

Now that I knew a jaded woman was the key to the whole thing, it all made perfect sense. And that slut who was hanging onto him was part of this thing too and I needed to let Lucas know that.

It occurred to me the pictures that were sent to me were sent by Torrance or Cecelia and I was sure they were from back when Iris and Lucas were a thing. And I didn't give him a chance to talk at all!

I shook it off and realized I was wrong. Lucas needed my help and I had to do something. I eased back into the front seat and turned the car on, staying very low in the seat so no one would really see me as I pulled out.

I was pretty sure Danny O'Brien, Lucas' driver, would be in one of his many cars parked in the back of the club, waiting for Lucas. I also knew there might be a chance Lucas had that tramp in the car with him doing something I might hate but I had to get to him no matter what.

And I planned on spraying my pepper spray right in that bitch's face when I saw her again. I had quite a few people on my shit-list and was trying to come up with a plan to bring them all down before they managed to do that to Lucas.

Easing my car around back, I saw Danny leaning against a black car I had never seen before but I knew it was him so I parked behind the car and got out of mine. Danny looked at me with a smile. "Hey, stranger."

"Danny, is Lucas in the car?" I asked. "Please tell me the truth. I know he might be with a woman but I've found out something very important and he needs to know this."

Danny took a few steps and opened the back door. "It's empty. He's still inside."

I pointed at the door at the back of the club and asked, "Is that how he usually comes out?" Danny nodded and I made my way to the door. Then something made me turn back and I asked, "Would you come with me?"

"I can't leave the car," he said. "But come here, real quick and let me in on what it is you want to tell him. Maybe I can be of some help."

Being unsure if Danny was involved or not, I decided I couldn't chance it. I shook my head and made my way inside the door and found myself in very dim lighting. It was a hallway then there was a set of stairs. So I took them.

The thumps of the hard beats from the music made the walls along the stairwell shake. I looked down at my bare feet and realized I had left my shoes off then decided I didn't care, I had to get to him.

When I saw Lucas the first time he'd been on the second floor and I knew chances were he'd be there again. So when I got to the door at the top of the stairs, I got ready to open it and see him with his hands all over another woman and steadied my temper to handle that. Lucas was clearly drunk and I should have treated him so differently before. Lucas doesn't get drunk. For all I know, that bitch drugged him.

Three men looked at me as I came into the balcony area. One came to me right away and said, "What the hell do you think you're doing? Sneaking in here?"

"No, I'm not sneaking, I'm looking for Lucas Montgomery. Have you seen him?" I asked as I peered around.

"He was up here a little while ago. He took a woman down to dance. He might be down there somewhere," the man told me then took a step back to allow me access to the balcony.

I could see the entire downstairs area and that's when I saw the blonde woman fighting with Lucas in a dark corner. He was holding the side of his head as she pointed around and it looked as if he was confused.

Finally, he started walking away from her and coming toward the stairs to come up to the balcony. She was following him and trying to hang onto him but he was looking very determined to get away from her.

I saw her reach into her purse and in a flash of gold, she hit him on the side of the head with what looked like a set of brass knuckles. He stumbled a little and shook his head. She pulled back to hit him again as he was looking on the wrong side of him for who had hit him.

But he regained enough balance to move forward and she missed him the second time. I waited for him to come up to me as he was effectively losing the woman as he made his way to the staircase. Then the door I had come in opened up and a large man was looking at my bare feet.

He made a few quick strides and had me in his arms quickly. "You're going back out the way you came, lady!"

I struggled and yelled, "I'm with Lucas Montgomery! Put me down!"

He didn't do what I asked, though. Instead, he took me all the way out and all the way to my car before he placed my feet on the ground. "This is not a place for you to park, miss. Get in the car and get the hell out of this area. Now!"

"But, I need to wait for Lucas!"

He opened the car door I had left unlocked with my keys in the ignition and crammed me back into my car. "Leave this area now or I'm getting the police."

So I decided to just do as he said. I didn't see Danny anywhere to get him to corroborate my attachment to Lucas so I decided it would be best just to go out to his estate and wait for him to show up.

As I drove back to the front parking area to leave the club, I saw that blonde bitch in the red dress coming out and making her way to the car Torrence and Cecelia were in.

Something just went insane inside of me and I threw the car into park and jumped out of it, racing to the woman who had no idea I was coming for her, I shrieked, "I know what you're doing! You'll never get away with it!"

Then I saw Torrence getting out of the little blue car and he shouted, "We have to get her before she tells Lucas!"

Suddenly the blonde woman, Torrence, and Cecelia were coming toward me, and Torrence had what looked like a bat in his hands. So I turned tail and ran back to my car and squealed past them, out of the parking lot. But Torrence managed to get one hit to my car with the bat. It broke my right headlight and now I was down to only one and I was driving as fast as I could.

In the rearview mirror, I saw them all getting back into the car and I was their new target for the night. It was me who could end their whole scheme and they were hauling ass in a car that was much faster than my little four-cylinder job.

It took no time at all for them to catch up to me. Then a gunshot made me jump and I couldn't believe what I saw when I looked into the rearview mirror. Cecelia was leaned out of it, holding a handgun.

I was fucked!

CHAPTER FOUR

Lucas

My head hurt like a son of a bitch and I had argued with that little tramp, Veronica, as I was sure she was the one who hit me but she insisted she hadn't. She told me there was some man who came out of the crowd and did it. She said she saw him and proceeded to pull me through the crowd to find him.

Something wasn't right and I could feel it. And all I could think about was getting to Sloan. As we got to a remote corner of the club, Veronica stopped leading me to the supposed man who had hit me and turned around. "Let's just get out of here. I can't find him. Come on. We can take my car."

With a frown, I said, "No. I'm going home. Without you."

I pulled away from her and found her hanging onto me like some kind of a freak as she shouted, "No! You're coming with me!"

Ignoring her, I easily kept walking then I finally felt her hand leave my arm. But only seconds later I was punched in the side of the head again. I looked back quickly and saw no one.

The punch seemed way too hard to have come from her but I wasn't going to take any chances. I ducked a bit and hurried to get to the stairs and away from the crazy woman.

My head was pounding from the two shots to it and I was stumbling most likely from the over consumption of the alcohol and the two hard blows. But I finally made it up the stairs and went to the exit door.

Three guys were hanging near it and one of them reached out and touched my arm. "Hey, you're Lucas Montgomery, right?"

"Yes," I said but shook him off and tried to keep walking.

"There was a woman looking for you," he said, making me stop.

"Black wig?" I asked.

He nodded. "But a bouncer carried her back out of here."

I pointed at the door not far from me. "Through there?"

He nodded and I hurried out the door and down the stairs. As I pushed open the exit door, I saw the car we'd taken to the club but I didn't see Danny. As I tried to open the door, I found it was locked.

"Fuck!"

I took my phone out and called Danny but it went straight to voicemail. I didn't feel like waiting around to find out what the fuck Danny had done so I called a cab, pissed as hell at how the entire night was going. Then I called Sloan and found I was still blocked. An idea popped into my head and when the cabbie got there, I asked if I could use his personal cell phone. After giving him a hundred for his trouble, he gave it to me and I tapped in her number.

It rang and after the second ring, she answered. "Sloan Whitlock here. I'm in a situation and can't talk right now."

I heard a gunshot then she screamed, "Shit!"

There was a series of bumps and rumbles then the phone went dead. My heart stopped. What the hell was going on?

I gave the cab driver Sloan's address and prayed that whatever was happening to her I'd find her on the way to her house. Then I thought I had better call the police too. I did hear gunfire and that should make it a top priority.

To be sure it was taken care of, I called Detective Allen. He sounded worried as he answered his cell, "Detective Allen, here." I could hear jostling and then the sound of car keys jangling then the sound of his engine starting up.

"This is Lucas Mont-"

"Montgomery! Where are you?" he asked as I heard his tires peeling out of wherever it was he was leaving in a hurry.

"I'm on my way to Sloan Whitlock's apartment. I think she's in trouble, I heard a gunshot when I called her but I lost the call."

"She called me, I'm on my way to her. I need you to go to the police station and stay there. I'll call the dispatcher and tell her to put you in my office until I have this all dealt with," he said as I heard more squealing tires.

"What's going on?" I asked as I couldn't even think straight.

"I can't talk. I have to drive. I have to get to her. I'll bring her to my office if she isn't hurt." He ended the call.

I didn't know what to think or how to make things better. "Take me to the police station instead," I told the cabbie. Then I saw a police car careening down the road that intersected the one we were traveling down. "Follow that car!"

"The police car, sir?" the cab driver asked. "Are you sure?"

I took out another hundred and dropped it on the seat next to him. "Yes, and if you can manage to stay close to him, I'll give you another when we get to where he's going."

The cabbie floored it and my phone rang. It was Danny. "Boss!" he said as I answered the phone.

"Danny, where the fuck are you?" I growled at him.

"Someone grabbed me. It took me a while but I got away. It was a couple of guys and I'm pretty messed up, Lucas. But I'm alive. I need to go to the hospital, though. I have a stab wound in my left side and another on my arm where I was trying to fend them off."

"What the fuck is going on?" I shouted. "Fuck! Do you have an ambulance coming for you?"

"I'm in the car. I'm going to drive myself. Sorry about the blood, Lucas. I promise to clean it up," he said but his voice was weak. I knew the man was strong as an ox but blood loss is stronger than any man.

"Pull over and call the ambulance, Danny. Do it!" I told him.

He made a little sigh then said, "I'll pull into this parking lot. I'll lock the car up and take the keys with me. I'll come back and get the car as soon as they let me out."

"God damn it, man!" I snapped. "Don't worry about that fucking car! I have tons of them. Call the ambulance then your wife and tell that mean bitch to get up there so she can be with you. Let me know what hospital they take you too so I can come up there as soon I have this other shit dealt with."

"Do I hear a siren, Lucas?"

"You do. I'll tell you all about it once I know what the fuck it's about. Now make the call, Danny." I ended the call before he could stall anymore.

Whoever was doing all of this was going too far. Going after my girl, my driver, and I think there was someone in that club after me. I never thought anyone would go to this length to ruin me. And why all the other people in my life.

I knew I needed to make one more phone call to let Torrence know what was happening. So I made that call and found him not answering me which was not like him at all. Before I could put the phone back in my pocket, it rang.

It was Torrence. "Hey, what's up?" he asked.

"Someone stabbed Danny," I said, hastily. "There seems to be someone after Sloan too. I think someone was after me at Club 9. And I'd like to know where my security is."

"Just calm down, Lucas," he said with a slightly aggravated tone which pissed me off even more.

"Calm down?" I shrieked at him. "You have no idea what's happening. Sloan is on the run from someone. She called the police and they're on their way to help her."

"They are?" he asked then I heard the phone make a clicking noise and I couldn't hear a thing. I knew he had put his phone on mute. Then there was another click when he came back on. "I need you to get somewhere secure. Maybe the person who's been after you has gone off the deep end. Your office is the most secure place I can think of. You need to get over there as quickly as you can. I'll come to you."

"No, I have to find Sloan. I'll be fine. I need you to try to find out who the hell is chasing her. I also need you to find out who the hell grabbed my driver and stabbed him."

"Danny was stabbed?" Torrence asked and I could tell he was speaking between gritted teeth.

"Yes, once in the side and on his arm. He's called an ambulance to take him to the hospital. Whatever this person wants from me, I need to know before anyone else gets hurt. If something happens to Sloan, I'll stop at nothing to make sure whoever is doing this meets their end," I said, seething with anger.

"Look, I know you're mad, Lucas. But you need to do what I'm telling you to. Go to your office," he said and then I heard a sneeze. A female sneeze.

"Who's with you?" I asked.

"No one," he said and his answer made me more than a little suspicious.

"I'll call you later," I said and ended that call before he could say anything else.

I knew something wasn't right. And I knew I had to get to Sloan. So we continued to follow the detective and I sat back and let my brain go to work on what the hell was happening and how I could stop it all before someone got killed.

My cell rang again and I saw it was from Danny's phone so I answered it, "How are you, buddy?"

It was his wife and she was screaming at the top of her lungs, "What the hell have you gotten my husband into? He's being taken into surgery and I swear to you Lucas Montgomery, I'll own everything you have if he dies for being involved with you!"

"Surgery?" I asked as my heart sank with the news.

"Yes!" she shrieked like a banshee. "What kind of shit are you into that has the people around you in danger? Shit! That poor young woman who you merely looked at in that club was nearly kidnaped just for that, Danny told me! So you better straighten your shit out or it'll be me who you have to worry about and I won't hide it. I'll just show up with a gun and blow your head off to stop anything else from happening to my husband. Do you hear me, Montgomery?"

"Fuck! Who didn't?" I told her. "I'm trying to take care of it. I'm going to tell the detective to keep an officer with Danny until this is settled. Make sure only a uniformed officer is guarding him and check the man's badge and make sure the name matches his ID. We can take no chances."

Her voice went soft as I could hear tears in her voice as she said, "Lucas, if anything happens to him, it will kill me. Please find out who's doing this and make it stop. I'm begging you."

"I will, I promise," I told her then ended the call.

The lights from the police car pulled to the side of the road and stopped. "Pull up right behind him," I told the cabbie.

"What is there's shooting?" he asked with a quivering voice.

"Then duck," I said. "I'll pay for any damages that might occur to your cab."

"Fuck the cab! What about damages to me?" he said.

"You too," I told him as he pulled to a stop behind the vehicle and I got out of the car.

Only Sloan's car was in front of the police car and she was bailing out and falling into Detective Allen's arms as she sobbed. My whole body tingled with shock as I saw blood pouring down her arm.

CHAPTER FIVE

Sloan

I had no idea I had been shot until I felt the blood trickling down my arm. I was sure it was just a flesh wound as there was no pain until I saw the blood, that is.

Once my eyes took in the red line making its way to my hand, which gripped the steering wheel so tight my knuckles were white, I felt a burning sensation near my shoulder.

Thankfully, not long after that, Torrence took a sharp left for some reason and I was left alone. I pulled over and started crying like a baby until the police car came up behind me. When I saw it was Detective Allen, I got out of the car and fell into his arms.

Then I heard a man's voice and looked up to find Lucas standing there. "Baby," he said.

I pulled out of the detective's arms and fell into Lucas' and cried out, "It's Torrence, Cecelia, and the little tramp you were with who were after me!"

Lucas' arms tightened around me as I heard the detective

say, "I'm calling an ambulance for her. And I'll get a team looking for Torrence."

"The car is blue," I said as I turned my head away from Lucas' chest.

Lucas shushed me and his hand ran over the wig and he pulled it off then pulled the stocking cap off me and used his fingers to comb my hair. "It's okay now, baby. I have you now."

"Lucas, I know who it is. I know who's behind the whole thing," I said through choked sobs.

"Good, baby. Let's get you to the hospital and taken care of then you can tell me and the detective everything," he said then picked me up and held me like a baby as I cried on his shoulder.

"I've never been more afraid," I said.

His lips pressed against the side of my head. "I know, baby. You hush now. Just rest. No one will ever hurt you again."

I tried to move my arm to run it around his neck but pain radiated all the way down it and I shrieked with the pain. "Fuck!"

"Keep it still, Sloan. You've been shot. You need to keep it still," he said with such a soothing tone it made me feel better.

"I'm sorry, Lucas," I whispered. "I'm sorry for not giving you a chance to explain things to me. Can you ever forgive me?"

"I already have. Do you think you can forgive me for bringing all this down on you, merely because I stared at you in that club one night?" he asked with a chuckle that shook his chest.

"I already have," I said. "I missed you more than I knew was possible."

"Me too, baby," he whispered. "Promise never to run off on me again."

"Never," I said. "Does that mean you still want me? And our agreement?"

"No," he said.

My heart stopped and my body started to ache. He didn't want me anymore. He may have forgiven me but he didn't want me anymore!

I couldn't speak as the ambulance pulled up and the paramedics had me on a stretcher in no time and in the back of the ambulance as Lucas stood there and watched with such sadness on his face it made me cry again. Not that I had stopped entirely.

He came to the doors and leaned in. "I'll take your car to the hospital. I'll be right behind you."

"Can't you come with me?" I asked as one of the paramedics put a huge needle into the vein on top of my hand, making me wince with the pain.

"Is he your husband or some other relative?" she asked me.

"No," I said as I looked at him.

"No one but family is allowed, sorry," she said.

"I'll take your car, Sloan," he told me. "And don't worry, I'll get to you."

I closed my eyes as some medicine she'd put into the IV she'd just attached took me over. "Okay."

Suddenly, nothing mattered. I guess the medicine was a mixture of pain reliever and calming agent. Whatever it was, I was feeling very relaxed. Finally, I was calm and the crying stopped.

My words were slurred when I said, "I really messed up. That man doesn't want to see me romantically anymore."

The paramedic looked at me with a frown. "For a man who doesn't want to see you anymore, he certainly didn't look like that. Don't worry about a thing right now. Just think about getting better. The bullet is lodged in your bicep. You're going to need a minor surgery to remove it."

"Fantastic," I murmured.

The rest of the ride was quiet and I kept drifting back and forth between being asleep and awake. Then I was being carried out of the ambulance and wheeled into a set of glass doors. There was a lot of chaos going on in the ER but I barely registered it.

My paramedic was on her little walkie-talkie, telling someone that I needed to be in the O.R. stat. Then I heard her say the bullet had lodged in the brachial artery and I would need immediate surgery.

"But it doesn't hurt that bad," I mumbled. "Are you sure it's not just a flesh wound?"

She smiled as she walked alongside of me, carrying the baggie with that wonderful drug in it. "I'm sure. But you'll be okay. You're just going to be taken right into surgery."

"Can I see Lucas?" I asked with a hoarse voice that felt odd as it came on quickly. "Is he here?"

"I have no idea," she said as she shook her head. "Even if he was, there's no time for visiting, I'm afraid. And they wouldn't let him back here, anyway. It'll be okay. You'll be out of surgery in a few hours and in recovery for a while then in a room of your own and he can come see you then."

"Why am I feeling so groggy," I choked out.

"Because I've already administered a bit of anesthesia to help you fall under more quickly when the anesthesiologist gets started on you." She looked up and smiled. "Here we are."

The stretcher pushed open a set of stainless steel doors and I found the room freezing cold. Several men were waiting for me in blue scrubs and face masks. Then one of them came up to my side and said, "Hi, I'm Doctor Stan. I'll be taking this pesky bullet out for you this evening. No need to worry, my dear."

"K," I muttered.

Two of the men came to me. One took my shoulders and one my feet and they picked me up and transported me to a very hard surface that was very cold. The thin sheet covering it did nothing to take the cold away from the obviously stainless steel operating table beneath it.

A man came up behind me and the smile he had shown in his blue eyes. "Hi, I'm Peter and I'll be your bartender for this evening. I'll be monitoring your vitals and keeping you sedated while he takes out that bullet. I can't imagine how a nice girl like you ended up being shot, but I bet you have a great story behind it."

"It's alright," I mumbled. "Nothing to write a book about."

He laughed and placed a clear thing over my mouth and nose and said, "Just take in normal breaths, and soon you'll be in La Land."

And just before I closed my eyes, I saw Lucas leaning his head against the glass at the top of the wall. Then I realized this was an operating theater and he was in the room, watching over my operation.

I raised my hand and gave him a little wave and he gave me one back then he blew me a kiss. My insides melted with the gesture and I thought for only a second that it meant he did still want to see me. Maybe he had changed his mind and was ready to go back to our agreement after all.

I hoped so, anyway.

Then it all went black and I fell under the spell of the drugs.

When I woke up, I felt stiff and my arm ached. It hurt worse than when I got shot. A moan came out of me as I tried to move. "Just be still," I heard a voice say.

It was his voice!

I laid perfectly still and blinked until my eyes focused. Then I saw him hovering over me as I lay in a hospital bed. I tried to talk but something stopped me and made me choke a little.

Suddenly his handsome face was gone and a female nurse

was there. She put her hand on my forehead as she said, "Let me get the tracheal tube out."

I gagged as something large slipped up my throat, making my eyes water. When it finally got out, I tried to talk and the sound was all scratchy. Lucas put his finger to my lips then the nurse pushed some button to raise the top portion of the bed up.

Lucas picked up a large cup with a lid and a plastic straw and held the straw to my lips. "Drink, slowly."

I did as he said to and felt the cool water go over my now very sore throat. After I popped the straw back out, I muttered, "Ow."

He smiled and kissed my forehead. Then the nurse took my attention as she began moving things around and calling for someone else over a little box on the bedside. "Now that you're awake, we can move you to your room. Mr. Montgomery here spared no expense and you're set up in one of our nicest rooms. He got another one of our very nice rooms for his driver, Mr. O'Brien. I'd say you two are pretty lucky to have this man looking out for you."

"Danny?" I croaked as I looked at Lucas.

"I'll tell you all about it later. Right now I want you to relax and heal, baby. No arguments about that. I'm going to take care of you," he said.

I felt better already, knowing he'd be there with me and for me. But I felt bad about hearing Danny was in the hospital too. An urgency leapt up inside of me as I had yet to tell Lucas the name of the woman behind everything.

"Lucas, the plot against you," I said but half the words didn't make it out audibly.

He patted my shoulder and said, "Don't worry. Your voice will be back by tonight and you can tell us everything you know then."

A male nurse came in wearing Scooby Doo scrubs and gave

me a smile. "Hello, I'm Leo and I'll be your nurse until the evening shift comes on." He took the bed and started moving me out of the tiny room and into a large hallway. "We're going all the way up to the top floor."

Into a large elevator, we went, with me on the bed and Lucas right beside me. I never felt safer than I did at that time. Lucas was like a rock and he was right there. He looked at me with something in his eyes I had never seen before. I wanted to call it love but this was Lucas I was talking about. Love wasn't even in his extensive vocabulary.

When the elevator stopped and we got off, my nurse pushed the bed along the wide hallway and into a large room already filled with flowers and get-well balloons. Tears stung my eyes as I knew Lucas had all of this done.

I mouthed a thank you to him and he smiled at me as the nurse placed my bed right in the middle and put a television remote next to my left hand. That's when I realized my right arm was immobilized. "Hey," I croaked. "What happened?"

The nurse sat on the left side of my bed and popped a thermometer in my mouth then set about to check my blood pressure. "Oh, honey! Let me tell you how lucky you are to be alive. That bullet was lodged in one of your very important arteries. When the doc took it out blood went everywhere. You had to have a few pints of blood transfused to keep you with us. Your hubby, here, gave the okay for the transfusion, otherwise, the doc couldn't have given it to you and the outcome could've been terrible."

He took the thermometer out of my mouth and I said, "Oh my!"

"Oh my, indeed!" the nurse said as he raised his eyebrows and took the blood pressure cuff off. "Your pressure is still on the low side but that's normal after surgery. I'm sure it'll come around in a few hours. Anyway, if there had been no one around to sign the papers, the doc would've had to do the surgery then bring you out of anesthesia to get your permission for the transfusion and then give it to you, if you agreed. It would've been very hard on your body."

All I could do was look at Lucas and mouth another, thank you. He was truly my hero.

CHAPTER SIX

Lucas

When the nurse finally left the room, I sat on the bed next to Sloan and ran my hand over her cheek. She looked so weak and helpless lying on that hospital bed. It was my lust for the poor thing that had her there and I knew that without a doubt.

"What do you want, baby?" I asked her. "Anything at all and I will get it for you."

She smiled, weakly and whispered, "Just you."

Just me is all she wanted and I was thinking very hard about giving her that. She'd wanted romance and I'd given her very little of that. The room was filled with flowers I had brought in and balloons and I had one more thing I wanted her to have but I was waiting for her to get more lucid before that happened.

The door opened and the detective came in. "I stopped by your office. Your head of security was in the secretary's office. Neither acted the least bit guilty when I talked to them about what happened last night. I told them Sloan had been incoherent when I got to her and couldn't tell me a thing. I also told them that she still hadn't woken up from the surgery to be able to point me in the direction of who it was who'd chased her and shot her. But when I asked Torrance if he could come to the station so we could talk more formally, he said he was unavailable anytime soon as he had a lot to do with a business risk you were having."

I looked down at Sloan as she spoke with broken words as some just weren't making it out of her mouth, "It was Cecelia who was shooting."

"Seriously?" I asked with surprise. I never saw that coming!

She nodded and I got her giant cup of water and held it to her lips. She took a drink then she said, "And the name of the woman behind it all is-"

The door opened again and there stood Drew Torrence. I wanted to fly off that bed and tear him limb from limb but the detective shot me a look that told me to stay calm. I knew we had to get more than just Sloan's testimony as to what she'd overheard to bring them all down.

Sloan gripped my hand and I felt her stop breathing. She was terrified and who could blame her. So I stroked her hair and whispered close to her ear, "You're fine. I'm here. Act like you don't remember a thing about the incident at all."

Her grip loosened a little as the detective asked Torrance, "What are you doing here? I thought you were way too busy to go anywhere."

"I need to talk to my employer." His dark eyes darted to mine. "Alone, it's about our leak."

"I'll come see you when I get time. Sloan is all I care about right now." I was not going to go somewhere alone with the man I knew tried to kill the woman in my life. The woman I had grown to love.

He shifted his weight and crossed his arms. "I really need to know what you want me to do, Lucas."

I wanted him to go jump off of a cliff but I didn't say that. "I tell you what, Drew, I give you permission to speak freely in front of these people. I know Sloan has nothing to do with this since she was nearly killed. And the detective is here to help. So go ahead and say what you have to say to me."

"Lucas, this room might be bugged," he said, still trying to get me to go somewhere with him. "Do you have any idea who was chasing you, Miss Whitlock?"

She shook her head and I answered for her, "She can't remember a thing about last night at all. I'm afraid the alcohol and the shock along with the anesthesia wiped her memory clean." He looked relieved with my lie and that's exactly how I wanted him to feel.

It was doubtful he'd do anything to harm me with the detective knowing I'd left the room with him, but I didn't trust myself not to harm him.

The detective took the reins and said, "There's no possible way this room is bugged. Only hospital workers have been in here."

"You never know," he said. "This information is too big to be found out. Or our guy might hear about how we're on to him and leave the country. Then we'll lose the chance to get him and stop this from happening again." He looked at me. "You do want this to end and never have any more threats, don't you?"

"Of course," I said. "But you seem to think you get to decide things and I told you to speak freely and you've argued with me which is an ignorant thing to do. So tell me what you have and the detective will make notes. Won't you, Detective Allen?"

He pulled out his phone and pressed a recording app. "I will. Start whenever you want to, Mr. Drew Torrence, I'll record it all."

Suddenly Drew was backtracking and seemed not to want to talk at all. Finally, he said, "I don't want this recorded. The man

I'm about to indicate in this is very powerful. If he found out it was me who ratted him out, then I'd be dealt with. If you know what I mean?"

The detective reminded him of something. "If this goes to court, which it will, then you'll have to testify anyway. So go ahead and tell Mr. Montgomery what you have to say."

"Do as he says, Torrence. It'll save me the trouble of telling him myself. I will have to handle this legally after all. So, please let us all in on who is behind this. Because now we have espionage, attempted kidnapping, and kidnapping charges, plus two counts of attempted murder to add to the ever-growing list of crimes this person and all who have helped this person will be charged with." I sat and stared at him as he fidgeted and squirmed under the pressure of all three of us scrutinizing him.

"You don't seem to understand. He will kill me." He paled a bit, getting into his act.

Sloan spoke quietly with a scratchy voice as she said one word, "Why?"

He narrowed his eyes at her then quickly stopped. "You wouldn't understand. You're young and naïve about the way the world works. I'm also checking in to find out who did this to you, Miss Whitlock."

She was quick to tell him, "Don't. The police are handling my attempted murder case. I'm not authorizing you to do a thing, Mr. Torrence. Stay out of my business."

He looked at me and asked, "Is that how you want it, Lucas?"

I nodded. "She's a grown woman and the decision is hers to make."

"I see," he said then began to back out of the room. "With the consequences that most likely will occur with my information, I don't want to reveal anything at this time."

The detective smiled. "That's your prerogative at this time. If

I need that information, I will have you picked up and brought in for questioning. You can bring a lawyer if you'd like."

Torrence nodded then looked at me. "Are you positive you don't want to let me tell you this in private? If you give the police the man's name, then I'm left out of it."

My eyebrows raised as I said, "Not very protective of you, is it?"

"Well, if I was going to handle this situation no police were going to be involved. I think you knew that, Lucas," he said.

"Well, they're involved now, aren't they," Sloan said. "And they're going to stay involved from now on."

"In all of it?" he asked me.

I gave him a nod and he looked afraid. It was the first time I saw fear in the man's expression. But I knew it wouldn't be the last.

He left the room and the detective put his finger to his lips and walked over to where Torrence had been standing. He pointed to the door handle and I went to look at what he was pointing at.

On the very back of the handle where no one would see, Torrence had placed a tiny bug. The detective took a picture of it but left it in place.

He gestured for me to follow him back to Sloan's bedside where he picked up the television remote and turned the T.V. on. I got the idea and said, "How about a little television, baby?"

She looked at me as I turned the sound way up. Then I leaned in and whispered, "He's placed a bug on the door handle. This is actually a good thing. We can lead him in the wrong direction and make a surprise attack."

She nodded and whispered back, "Give me a pen and paper and I'll write down everything."

I decided to make small talk while the detective thought about what we should say to throw them all off. "Too bad about your memory, Sloan. But I have to tell you that I'm not all that upset about it. You and I had a little fight and that's a good thing you don't recall any of that."

"Why'd we fight?" she asked and winked at me.

"Never mind," I said as I found a small pad of paper and a pencil. I pulled up the tray-like table they had in the room that went over her bed and placed the pencil in her left hand and the paper on the tabletop. "I want you to think about nothing. It's more important to me that you get well."

The detective came up with some information that was true and made it seem as if we'd never find the culprit who shot Sloan. "I pulled up some traffic cameras and we got the plates of a small blue car that was following you through several stop lights. But the plates didn't belong to that car. They belonged to one the perpetrators got off a car in a junkyard."

"Were you able to see how many people were in the car or if they were men or women," I asked.

"It was too dark to make anything inside the car out. The streetlights glared off the windshield, making it impossible to make out anyone," the detective said as Sloan was having a bit of trouble writing with her left hand.

Then she stopped and looked at me with concern. "Lucas, I have to get my thesis done. How can I do it if I have no use of my right hand? I'll never get to graduate this year. I'll have to go longer."

I wrapped my right hand around her left one to steady it as I said, "I'll get you some help. I'm sure, given the circumstances, your professor will allow you to have someone to type as you dictate."

"I hope you're right," she said as she formed the first letter. It was an, 'L' and then she managed to get out an, 'I' and before I knew it, the name, 'Lila' was on the little notepad.

I had no clue who that was. So I helped her with the last

name and when I saw that it was Sheffield, it finally dawned on me who the woman was.

A one - night stand and a difficult woman to take. Lila was the cousin of Iris and I had no idea why she'd want to take me down so bad, she'd kill people to do it.

I wrote down the town she lived in upstate New York and the detective gave me a nod and said, "Well, I'll leave you two alone. If I get any information, I'll let you know, Mr. Montgomery."

"Thank you, detective," I said as I walked him to the door. "And I'll let you know if I find anything out as well."

"Good deal. We need to bring these people to justice," he said.

"That we do," I agreed and we shook hands then he left.

I needed a place no one knew about to take Sloan when she was released. It needed to be big enough for me to keep Danny and his wife and kids there too. I had no other people in my life worth hurting.

But now that we had the name of who was masterminding everything, the time was getting much closer and I had to do some fast planning.

CHAPTER SEVEN

Sloan

Two days passed and Danny and myself were being released from the hospital. Lucas was able to stay away from his office as he told the staff he wouldn't be leaving my side until I was completely able to take care of myself again.

The trap had been baited, Lucas and the detective worked together and finally, they found some bank accounts for Torrence and Cecelia that weren't on file with his office. With the cooperation of the president of the bank the accounts had been drawn on, they found twelve people who Lila Sheffield made deposits to.

It seemed she'd been the one to set all of the accounts up for the individuals using a computer at her company's headquarters. Not in her office, of course. But only two doors down in another lowly employee's office, she'd done her dirty work.

What's worse is she used that poor woman's work computer to make solicitations for people who wanted to do some undercover work for her. She was setting up that woman to take the heat of what she was behind. But thankfully, Lucas was much smarter than she was.

The day we left the hospital, we were taken to someone's home the detective knew and the family was gone for the week. Lucas made sure Torrence was off on a wild goose chase so we wouldn't be followed. He'd told Lucas we were all going to his estate until Danny and I were better.

Detective Allen met us at the modest home in a suburb no one would ever look for a billionaire in. We sat in the living room that evening as he filled us in. "The videos from the traffic cameras have been enhanced by our team of professionals and we can see the people in the front seat. All the way to the gun in Cecelia's hands."

"Are there any of her leaning out of the window to shoot me?" I asked as I sat next to Lucas and he held me close to him.

With a smile, the detective pulled a package of 8 by 10 photos out of his briefcase and handed Lucas the pictures. They were clear as day and there were three of Cecelia hanging out the window and fire coming out of the end of the pistol.

The next pictures were from the outside cameras at Club 9. The tramp, who I found out called herself Veronica was seen getting into the car with them. There were also pictures from inside the club and it showed her hitting Lucas both times and even the third time when she missed. It was all there in color photographs. The bank records indicated the rest. And it was all about to go down on them all.

The police were ready for the battle that would surely come along with the capture of Torrence. He had an arsenal and many men to protect him after all. So Lucas had made sure to separate him from them at the specific time the officers were going to make the arrests, simultaneously.

A little lie was what Lucas told Torrence. He asked him to go out to his estate so they could talk. Where he would not be, but the police would. He'd made sure the staff was out of there but that their cars were there so Torrence wouldn't get suspicious and flee the set up.

Detective Allen stayed with us so we would know everything as it happened as he had the radio channel on all of the policemen had theirs on to coordinate the plan. I held Lucas' hand and leaned my head on his shoulder as we waited for information to come in.

He kissed the side of my head and whispered, "I can't wait for this to be over and things can get back to normal for us."

We hadn't talked at all about our arrangement or lack thereof. There was just no privacy and the fact was I felt too weak to get into any kind of drama. Any more than I was already in.

The detective's radio made a squealing noise then a man was talking, "The target is on the premises of the Montgomery estate, stay alert."

My body went tense with his words and Lucas ran his hand up and down my arm. "its okay, sit back and relax."

I tried to do what he said but I was on pins and needles. I had an idea that Torrence wasn't going to be an easy capture. But Lucas assured me that the team inside of his home was a swat team. He would be taken in even if they had to kill him.

I really didn't want any more bloodshed than had already occurred. I wasn't an eye for an eye kind of person. I just wanted Lucas safe. I was falling in love with the man. He might never want me the same way, as he hadn't tried to give me any kind of intimate kiss or touch. So I was unsure what he and I would have once it was all over.

We heard the sound of the doorbell ring at the estate and the officer who was officiating that arrest whispered, "Stacy get the door."

The detective let us in on who Stacy was. "That's a female

officer. She's wearing one of the maid's uniforms to throw him off. Our men are stationed just inside the two rooms off of the hallway the door leads into."

His radio went off again as another officer said, "We're about to enter the front of Lila Sheffield's residence. She is inside according to our intel."

Another officer came over the radio. "We are just outside the office of Lucas Montgomery and we have a visual on our target."

Lucas looked pissed and hissed, "I can't believe her. Out of all of them, I can't believe she'd do this."

He was hurt by Cecelia more than anyone else. She was a magnificent actress, I had to give her that. But I felt so bad for those kids of hers. Lucas had promised me he'd take care of finding their father and making sure they were taken care of. Her three kids were at school that day. Their little worlds were about to be turned upside down and my heart hurt for them all.

The last person they were picking up was Veronica. She worked at a strip club and the officer in charge of her arrest made his presence known. "We're going into the Leopard Lounge now."

The sounds of all the men talking on the radio were confusing as they all had their intended perpetrators and all were shouting commands to lie on the ground and put hands behind heads. Then a loud buzzing sound happened and one of the officers said, "He's immobile, cuff him."

Detective Allen smiled. "They had to use the Taser on Torrence, it sounds like."

"I hope they hit him in the balls," Lucas said, harshly. "That man has it coming to him."

I laughed a little. "A bit barbaric, are we?"

The way he looked into my eyes made my heart stop. "Where you're concerned, definitely."

He didn't look like a man who was about to let me go the way

I thought he might be thinking about doing with this thing finally over. He looked at me like he wanted me around for a long time.

One after the other, we heard the arrests being made and Lucas had the judge who would set their bond in his hip pocket so the amounts for each of their bond would be outrageous since most of them had a lot of money.

The feds were busily working to freeze their assets with the arrests made and things were clicking into place. With the news of the last arrest of Lila, the detective told us we were free to go home. Those people were no longer threats to any of us.

We left that house and climbed into the back of limousine Lucas had picked us up in at the hospital and back we went to Washington to start living our lives normally.

Danny and his wife, Lane, were pretty damn happy to be getting back home. As we dropped them off first, they gave us both hugs before getting out. "It'll be great to get back to work, Lucas."

"You're taking a month long vacation. You let me know where you want to go and I'm setting it all up. I'm going to cover every expense. Plus, you're getting a bonus. And Lane's getting a new car. You call my dealer up and have him bring you a few of the one's you might be interested in."

Lane covered her mouth with her hands as tears sprang up in her eyes. "Oh, Lucas! I'm sorry I threatened to kill you that day!"

"No hard feelings," he said.

I looked at him with surprise as the door closed after they got out and we were off to I supposed my apartment to drop me off. "She said she was going to kill you?"

"Yes, but I never believed her," he said then took my hand and pulled it to his lips. His soft lips pressed against it and it made my insides flutter. "I want to ask you something, Sloan."

He moved to get on one knee in front of me and my heart stopped. I couldn't speak as he pulled out something from his pocket. When he opened his hand I saw a ring inside of a small black box.

"Lucas," I said in a whisper.

"Shh," he said. "I made a phone call after getting your parents' number from your cell phone. I asked your father for his permission and I got it. So I'd like to ask you, Sloan Rivers Whitlock, if you will make me the happiest man in the world and become my wife?"

I think it was shock that filled me and had me unable to say a word. I just stared at that gorgeous and huge rock then I looked into this eyes. A lump was in my throat and I had to swallow three times to make it go down as he waited patiently for my answer.

Still, my words wouldn't come out. He started to frown and my heart told me to hurry up. "Yes!"

His frown turned into a smile and he took the ring out of the box and slid it onto my shaking finger. "Thank God! You had me worried for a minute."

"I couldn't speak, I was overwhelmed, not thinking about whether I should marry you or not."

He sat next to me again and pulled me into his arms. "Thank you. Thank you so much, Sloan. You have no idea how much I love you and I'm going to prove it to you every single day of our lives."

His hand moved up the side of my neck then he cupped the back of my head and gave me the first real kiss he'd given me in over a week. My mouth opened and invited him right in as our tongues said their hellos.

My body ignited with the kiss I'd missed so damn much, it hurt. And we were going to get married and one day have babies and there would be little him's and me's running around the estate.

I ended the kiss abruptly as it all came crashing in on me. "Your society will not make this easy on you, Lucas. Just look how they treated me at that charity event. Oh, no. They'll never accept me as one of their own. This is a mistake you're making. I'm not worthy!"

He took my face in his hands and made me look at him. "You are never to talk like that again. You are soon to be Mrs. Lucas Montgomery and people will respect you simply because of that. No reason to worry. And if a soul is misfortunate enough to utter one word about you, I suppose you know I'll have them publicly stoned for the offense."

I laughed at his over the top words. He could be so funny when he wanted to be. But he was most likely right about me just having his name making people look at me differently. It might make them see me as being on their level.

God I hoped so, anyway!

CHAPTER EIGHT

Lucas

My heart was pounding. I couldn't believe my ears. There was a part of me that thought she'd tell me, no. I knew she felt out of her element with the people I rubbed elbows with but she could get used to them and their eccentric ways.

"So, move in with me," I said next.

She looked at me with wide, brilliantly green eyes and shook her head. "What about my roommate, Randi? She can't make the rent and all the bills on her own?"

"I'll make sure your part is covered until she finds someone else to room with." I ran my hand along her shoulders and pulled her tight to me. "I not only want you with me, Sloan. I need you with me."

The way her eyes darted back and forth told me she was thinking about it. "Will you give me time to do my thesis and whatever else I need to do?"

"I'll give you your own office, baby," I told her as I hugged her. "Whatever you need or want, you will get it. I just want you with me."

"Randi's probably going to be pissed at me," she said.

So I threw in something extra, "I'll send one of my maids over to clean the apartment once a week and do all of her laundry. I'll also give her a brand new car. Whatever kind she wants."

"Wow!" she said as she nodded. "Now that might help soften the blow. Okay, I'll move in with you then. How can I say no and cost Randi all of that good stuff?"

So I sat back and held her in my arms and felt better than I ever remembered feeling. She was going to be with me every night and each morning. I was hooked on her like I didn't know was possible. I had been fighting it but nearly losing her made me see time was a gift and I needed to be a hell of a lot more appreciative of that.

Our first night back home had us watching some television in bed as I fed her some crackers and cheese so she'd have something on her stomach when she took her pain meds. I had become a nursemaid, a thing I never knew I was good at. But like most things, I figured out what needed to be done and developed a plan to do it and became great at it.

Her sweet red lips parted to accept the food I placed against them. Her eyes twinkled as she took the bite and then she sighed. "You're really sweet when you put your mind to it."

"So are you," I said then gave her a sip of water.

She gave me a smile. "I'm always sweet."

"I'm not about to argue with you," I said with a laugh.

I think we both knew she had a short fuse but who was I to bring that up? Especially since I wanted to keep her calm and happy. After one more cheese covered cracker, I handed her the pill to ease her pain.

She handed the glass of water back to me after taking the pill and said, "Lucas, do you think we could have sex? I mean, I'll have to pretty much lie still since my right arm is immobilized but I feel up to it."

"Have sex?" I asked as I tweaked her nose. "Nah, I don't think so."

Her frown made me laugh, so I started unbuttoning the pajama top she had on. "I think we should make love."

Her lips quirked up into a sideways smile. "You had me worried there for a minute."

"That's fair, don't you think? Since you took so long to accept my marriage proposal?" I asked her as I peeled the silk shirt off of her, being very careful of her arm.

She nodded and ran her hand over my bare chest. "Um, hm. I have missed touching you so much. You have no idea."

"I have every idea. If you knew how badly I wanted to climb into that hospital bed with you."

"You should have. I wanted you to. I didn't want to ask, though," she said as her hand moved all the way down to the top of my pajama bottoms.

I got off the bed and dropped them then pulled hers off too and looked at her perfectly wonderful body. When my eyes had traveled all the way up her body, our eyes met. "You're gorgeous."

She smiled. "So are you. Now show me what these nights are going to be like now that we're engaged."

I ran my hands up her silky legs. When we bathed together before bed, I had shaved them for her, using an expensive shaving cream and the effects were stunning. "Like silk," I said as I ran them all the way up to her knees. Then bent them and leaned in to kiss her sweet spot.

Her moan made me hard in an instant. One of her feet moved over my back as she lifted her ass up for more. She wasn't that girl anymore who worried about having more than one orgasm. Now she was ready to have as many as I could give her.

I wasn't planning on being too vigorous with her that night.

She was fragile and I had to remember that. No matter how excited I got, I had to remember she'd been shot only two days before. But her body was calling to me and so was her mouth. "Baby, show me you love me."

My stomach tensed with her words. We'd barely started using them and each time I heard the word, love, come out of her mouth it gave me such an intense reaction. My lips grazed her sex as I whispered, "I love you, Sloan."

Then I gave her pert pearl a nice long lick then wrapped my lips around it and sucked it gently. The sound she made gave me chills. I loved the little sounds she made while I pleasured her. She really got into it and it made it so much sweeter.

I picked her up, cupping her ass cheeks in both hands. Loving the way they were firm yet soft and supple. I kneaded them like dough, making her purr and wiggle her hips up to me.

My intimate kiss deepened as I ran my tongue through her wet and warm folds until I found her hot canal and thrust my tongue into its wet, salty depths. Her back left the bed as she arched up and made a fantastic gasp. "Yes!"

Her left hand moved through my hair as I tongue fucked her until she was screaming my name and sending her hot fluids to meet my hungry tongue. I couldn't stop, I had to drink her in. Her moaning and screaming continued as she pulled at my hair. Her body was mine and there was no denying it.

As my mouth left her sweet heat, I kissed my way up her body. Her legs wrapped around me as I slipped into her. We both groaned with agonizing relief to feel one another this way again. "Oh, God!" I moaned as I felt like I was home. "A week is far too long to stay away from this feeling."

Her hand moved over my back as her lips pressed against my neck. "It is. What you do to me is amazing."

I eased up then back down and pulled back to look at her. "Are you okay? I'm not hurting you, am I?"

"Not one bit," she said as she bit her lower lip. "Now take me, Lucas. Make me only ours forever."

"Oh, baby, you have no idea how I've wanted to hear that," I growled. Her body was reacting to mine with a heated passion I didn't recall her having before. I guessed it was the now permanence of our relationship that had her so hot and intense.

Whatever it was, I liked it. She arched as I thrust and we both made sounds we'd never made before. Her insides grabbed me and pulled me into her as I ground my hard cock into her.

She started into a climax and I stayed the course. I intended to see her through at least one more. Her nails dug into the flesh of my back as she gripped me tightly around the waist and wailed like a banshee with the release.

It spurred me on and I went faster and harder as her breaths went from harsh to ragged and she squirmed underneath me. Her wiggling sent me over the edge. I couldn't stop the need to give into her. I spilled my juices into her as my body shook with the release.

It had been only nine days since I had been with her but it had felt like an eternity and now I had her. The ring was on her finger and all that was left was to put that all important gold band on both of our fingers to make sure what we had stayed secure.

With sporadic breaths, I whispered, "I'm never letting you go."

"Not even when I get all mad about something?" she asked with a tired smile on her beautiful face. Her cheeks were flushed with the exhilaration and she glowed with love.

I couldn't help myself. I rolled off of her and laid on my side as I caressed her hot cheek. "Not even when you lose that awful temper of yours, baby. I love you. You're stuck with me."

She laughed and pulled one of my fingers into her mouth and gave it a naughty little suck. "I think I'd like to be stuck with you. As long as you let me be me. I can't have you thinking just because you make me your wife that means you get to control me. That's not part of the deal."

"Not even a little?" I asked as I kissed her alabaster shoulder. "Cause a little control isn't bad, is it?"

She ran only the tip of her finger along my top lip as she looked into my eyes. "Not even a little. And I promise not to control you either. As a matter of fact, I want us to write our own vows. That honor and obey crap isn't a thing I can agree to."

"Well, you can agree to honor me. I'll always honor you." I ran my finger over her taut nipple, igniting a low moan from her sweet lips.

It went erect and she licked her lips. "You're going to always honor me? Well, then I should return that, shouldn't I?"

Leaning over, I took her nipple between my lips and rolled at as my hand laid on her stomach. It went tight as she ran her hand through my hair and let out another moan.

Releasing her tasty tit, I said, "And I will obey some of the things you ask of me. The important things like don't screw around with other women and don't be mean to you."

"And don't forget the most important one, Lucas," she said as she pulled at my nipple, making it pucker and making my dick pulse. "You'll always put the toilet seat down."

I laughed and said, "Of course, I'll obey that cardinal rule. I'm not trying to get my ass chewed out after all."

Her lips were barely parted and it made me want to kiss her so badly. When I took her mouth she ran her hand around my neck and held me to her.

The way her lips began quivering had me pulling back and I found tears in her pretty eyes. "What is it, baby?"

She blinked a few times as I wiped the tears off of her cheeks. "I can't believe this is real. I could never have even dreamed that I'd end up with a man like you. This can't be real.

I'm a nobody from the middle of nowhere and you are a man with a lot of money, power, and class. I don't deserve."

I kissed her again to stop her from saying anything else. When I ended the kiss, I looked into her eyes and said, "I am the one who doesn't deserve you. Even though that's completely true in every sense, I'm going to have you. You and I will never walk a step behind each other. We will go through this life, hand in hand, and be complete partners in this life. I love you and your hard-headed, stubborn, and completely loveable ways. You're an inspiration to me and I'll be proud to call you my wife."

Then she burst into tears which she said were all happy ones and I made love to her again to get her to quit crying and start making those sexy sounds I loved to get her to make.

Our life would be great. I had not even one doubt about that.

CHAPTER NINE

Sloan

A year after our marriage was official with a nice little wedding in my hometown with only a few friends and family members to witness it all, we were about to start our family.

I had graduated and started a nice little job with one of the poorer school districts in Washington. I was determined to figure out how to get those kids who needed a lot more than what life had dealt them more of everything.

More attention, love, choices, advantages and most of all education. And I was pleasantly surprised when Lucas helped me with everything I wanted to implement without bossing me around.

He did exactly what he'd told me he'd do. He treated me as his equal. He listened to me and instead of talking down to me when he had an idea that might work a little better, he talked to me about things. Lucas had a mind that was much like a machine. He was incredible and I'd have been a complete idiot not to listen to him and implement some of his great ideas.

Together, we were becoming a power-couple. But the good kind, not the kind who are out to get things. We became the kind who got things done for others. It made me feel great when I passed people on the street who knew of our efforts to help others.

I could pass another billionaire and get a smile and a nod as well as the poorest person in town and get the same nod and smile. It was all going so much better than I ever thought it would. And now we were ready to start our own little family.

Well, little isn't really how I'd describe it. Lucas wanted to have at least four children. And when he told me about how lonely it was for him, growing up as an only child, it made my heart ache. So I agreed to the magic number four as he further explained that he'd been reading some of my old college school books and finding out that even numbers of children got along better than odd numbers.

How could I not agree with him?

So I beat him home that night and was lying on our big bed with a bottle of his favorite wine on the bedside table and me in a naughty negligée. It was a deep green color, his favorite color on me. It had a plunging neckline and was short. It covered just to the bottom of my bottom. I left the panties off because who likes panties, anyway.

I'd let my hair down and thanks to being rich and being able to spend loads of money on hair care products, my red mess had finally been tamed.

My cell rang and I picked it up to see it was Lucas. "Hey, you," I answered.

"I'm sorry, baby. I'm going to be late. The damn board members have their panties in a bunch over an overseas deal they think is a bad idea. I have to deal with them. This might go late into the night," he said, wrecking my sexy mood.

"Oh, man!" I said as I was thoroughly disappointed.

"Did you have something you wanted to do?" he asked.

"Um, yeah," I said as we had discussed this just last night. "I wanted to make a baby with you. If you do recall?"

"Oh that," he said with a laugh. "We can do that anytime. It's not a big deal."

Not a big deal?

"Wow! I mean, wow! Lucas, we just talked about this and you decided the damn board members are going to come between us on this specific night? I'm not about to pretend that I'm not pissed about this. I don't see why that meeting can't wait until tomorrow! And what do you mean by we can do that anytime? This is supposed to be special, damn it!"

The bedroom door burst open and there stood my husband, tugging his expensive suit off as he came in the door. He was laughing and tossed his phone on the dresser. He kicked the door closed and looked me over. "Very nice. And I love that heated color in those pretty little cheeks of yours."

"What the hell did you do that for?" I yelled at him. "You made me all pissed off for no damn reason."

"Oh, I had my reasons, baby. You're a wildcat when you get mad and I haven't seen that side of you in a while. Everything has been going your way so much, I missed that spark you get when you're mad." He'd completely undressed by the time he'd stopped talking and my temper was even hotter when I found out he'd done that just to rile me up.

I hopped up on my knees on the bed and starting wagging my finger at him as I yelled, "Well, now I'm really mad!"

He just started chuckling and smiling. "You're so damn cute when you get mad."

"I'm going to show you cute, buddy!"

"I know you are," he said. His hands went to my waist as he lifted me up. I kicked my feet and screamed. "Easy, red. You're going to blow a gasket."

Our bodies touched as he brought me back down then he kissed me hard, his hand held the back of my neck so I couldn't back away from him. I wanted to stay mad but I couldn't. When he kissed me it took all the fight out of me.

So I wrapped my legs around his waist as he walked to the end of the bed. The kiss grew as he laid me on the end of it. His cock was swelling as he ground it against my core. I arched up to get him to fill me but he pulled back. "On your knees," he said with an air of authority.

He knew I hated that tone but in the bedroom, I quite liked it. My eyes went wide. "Are we establishing our dominance in the bedroom, Lucas?"

"I am," he said. "So hurry up and do what I said."

Eyeing him all the while, I moved around on the bed until my ass was facing him. It was then I realized something that had gone unnoticed in the monster-sized room I'd called our bedroom for well over a year. A large mirror filled the wall and I could see us both in it.

The dim light of the candlelit room made Lucas glow a golden color as he stood behind me. His handsome face was pulled into a smile. "You like the new mirror I had installed today?"

I nodded. "I have to say I do. And I have to confess I didn't even notice it until it was filled with your gorgeous reflection." His hand moved over my ass and I felt it but could also see it in the mirror. It made the feeling more intense and I went wet with just that."

"I thought it would be nice if we both could see everything while we made our baby." He leaned over and kissed the top of my left butt cheek as I watched him in the mirror. It made me moan and my body began to ache.

"I think you had a very good idea, hubby," I said as I continued to watch him and feel him at the same time.

He leaned over me, not making any penetration but everything was touching me. His chest on my back felt warm and he pulled my hair away from one side of my neck and ran his teeth up the long column.

His dark hair fell over the side of his face as I watched him nip and suck my neck. All I could do was watch how gracefully he moved his body along mine. His hands dipped at my waist as he pulled back and ran his hands along me as he did.

My sides quivered as his hands stopped at my waist and he pulled me back until his hard cock was between my ass cheeks. It was straight up, only the side of it was between them and when he started pumping against my rectum it sent a mix of fear that he was about to stick it into me and hope that he was about to stick into me.

I closed my eyes with the new sensation and his hand connected with my ass. "Eyes open!" came his order. "I want to see those gorgeous green eyes all the while I take you."

I nodded and smiled. "Got it, boss."

He smiled back and continued to stimulate my ass in a way I didn't know I'd like. As he pumped away, he looked at me through the mirror and sucked two of his long fingers. He placed them on my clit and began rubbing it until it was hard as a rock. The combination of actions had me on fire.

When his fingers went inside of me, I felt my walls gripping him. I wanted more than just his fingers but if that was all he was allowing me at that time then I was going to come all over them.

I rocked back on him, our bodies moved back and forth in a rhythmic motion. I started shaking as the orgasm crested inside of me. He smiled and moved his fingers out of me and put his hands on my shoulders, pressing down until they were on the bed and my ass was high up in the air.

His nails raked down my back as he stood back up and then his large, hot cock was thrust into me with one hard movement. He stayed perfectly still while my orgasm moved my body around his cock. I felt it pulsing inside of me and it made my orgasm go on and even grow in intensity. I was a squealing mess of pure pleasure.

Once my walls had stopped convulsing around him, he pulled his cock back slowly. His hands went to my hips and his eyes met mine in the mirror. "I want you to wait until I tell you to come. I want us to climax together."

"Okay, that sounds good to me too," I said as I bit my lip and hoped I could hold it back.

That wasn't a thing we practiced. He allowed me to climax as many times as my body needed to. But he was right. Making a baby was different from everyday sex. It needed to be memorable. It needed to be more about us coming together to bring another life into this world.

No one could ever accuse Lucas of being unemotional. He may seem stiff and unmoved in the boardroom, but in the bedroom and when we had our intimate moments, he was full of emotion and so caring it was nearly unreal.

His movements were slow and deliberate at first. He was easing into me as we held each other's eyes but mine kept drifting to watch his muscular body move behind mine. He stopped for a second and lifted me up and took a few steps to move us where the mirror would catch our reflections from the side.

Now I could see his massive dick going in and out of me and I was mesmerized. His large cock moved into me and came out with a slick shine of the wetness from inside of me. I watched his hand gripping my waist then he slid it down and ran it over my ass.

I groaned with the need to feel his hand all over my ass. He lifted his hand and brought it down with a nice smack and I moaned. He smiled. "You got even wetter."

"It makes me hot as hell when you do that." I licked my lips and hoped he'd do it again.

When Lucas was being dominate in the bedroom, he didn't allow me to tell him what to do to me. Any other time I could but when he played this role I was to be quiet and accept the pleasure he decided to give me. It was a thing I loved to do now and then. It made me feel a little kinky and very hot. Like he was a cave man and I was his cave woman. And as long as we both liked it, then it was going to continue to occur from time to time.

CHAPTER TEN

Lucas

On a Monday in July, my wife had our first child, a son. I watched her go through a pretty tough delivery and she took it like a champ. Sure, she had to bitch out a nurse who wasn't listening to her when I went to the car to grab some blanket she'd become attached to. I had to smooth her ruffled feathers and apologize to the nurse.

But Sloan calmed down pretty quickly with a kiss from me and the blanket wrapped around her, then apologized for losing her temper. I held her hand through it all and when our son made it out into the world, we kissed. A sweet kiss that told me more than words ever could.

Sloan loved me. She'd just pushed this eight-pound kid out of her body that I had helped put there and she wasn't one bit upset about it. She loved me that damn much!

"I love you," I told her as I stroked her red cheek. "You were awesome."

"Thanks," she said. "It was pretty hard. But looking at you made it all worthwhile. I love you, Lucas Montgomery."

Her smile was radiant and her eyes were glassy with unshed tears. When our son was held up so we could see him those tears fell like rain and I found some brimming up in mine too. But I wiped them away so I could cut our new son, Jackson's, umbilical cord.

His cries made my heart hurt and I asked the doctor, "Is he crying because this hurts him?"

She shook her head. "He's just crying because this is all new to him and he's cold and afraid. It's going to be up to you guys to let him know it's all good and you're going to keep him safe for the next eighteen years or so."

After his cord was clamped off and cut, he was wrapped in a little blue blanket and a blue cap was placed on his head and he was placed into my waiting arms. The way he stopped crying immediately had the whole room going, "Aww."

My first words to him were, "Hi, little buddy. Daddy has you now. It's all going to be okay. I picked you out the perfect momma and she and I are going to take care of you and love you forever."

Sloan laughed and said, "I thought it was me who picked out the perfect daddy for him."

I moved to her side and held the baby down for her to see him. She ran her hand over his chubby cheek. "We both know it was me who picked you out, Sloan. Out of a crowded night club with tons of eligible women, I caught site of you and I knew you were something else. You were special."

She sniffled as a tear rolled down her cheek. "I'm pretty glad I caught your eye. We made us one cute kid here."

I kissed her cheek as the nurse came to take the baby to do all of the vital stuff they do to babies. Then I let him go and turned my attention to his momma. I ran my hand through her hair and smiled at her. "Sorry about the attempted kidnapping, and the kidnapping."

She laughed, "Don't forget about the shooting."

I laughed too. "How could I forget that?" I pressed my lips to hers then said, "But you stayed with me. It seemed like the world was against the two of us getting together but you kept on staying tough and making the decision to keep on seeing me."

"Except for that one week," she said as she took my chin into her hand. "That horrible week."

"The longest week on record," I said as I looked into her red-rimmed eyes. "Thank you for coming back to me. Thank you for marrying me and thank you for giving me a son. Our first one. Thank you for loving me, Sloan. This life would be nothing without you. I could lose every dime I have and as long as I have you, and now that little guy over there, then I'd be the richest man in the world and would never want anything more than your love."

I heard a sniffle from across the room and looked up to find one of the nurses wiping her eyes. She noticed me looking at her and said, "Oh, Lord! I'm sorry. I didn't mean to be listening. It's just that you said that so well and it was obvious that you really meant it and, damn, I'm sorry. I just wish I'd have held out for a man who loves me the way you love this lady right here."

Sloan looked at the young woman and offered her a little wise advice. "The way to get this kind of love is to give it. If you knew how hard both of us tried not to fall in love, you'd be amazed. This whole thing started out as lust then it turned into more than that. And when the chips were down, we held tight to each other. That's where true love is made. It's made in the trenches as life hurdles things at one or both of you and you hold onto one another for dear life. Because the thought of losing them is too much to think about."

I heard another sniffle and found another nurse with tears. "You too?" I asked with a chuckle.

"It's just that what she's saying is so true and yet I never thought about it like that. My husband and I have been married for fifteen years. And the last three have been miserable. We even talked about separating but neither of us really want to move on to anyone else. And after listening to you two, I think all we really need is to remember what's real. Why we got together in the first place. It was to join forces to make it through this life with a partner. Somewhere along the line, we forgot that. But I'm going to make a date with that old man of mine tonight and try to change that."

"That's good to hear," I said. "I'm sure we'll have our rough patches but when you hold on through the times others would be saying goodbye and good riddance to one another you gain a little something."

"Connection," Sloan said. "You gain a connection you didn't have before. You realize that person went through something pretty bad and instead of busting you up, they clung to you, they trusted you. A connection is made and it grows and grows until you feel like two parts of one whole." Her hand gripped my arm as she looked up at me. "There are no better halves, there is just this one whole being who has two bodies, souls, hearts, and works together to make life livable."

I kissed her cheek as the women watched and knew our lives would continue to go well. I knew, without a single doubt, that Sloan and I could get through anything, after all we'd been through.

"Only three more to go," she said.

"What?" I asked perplexed.

"Three more pregnancies," she said.

Then the baby started crying again and the nurse looked at us with a laugh. "Seems this little guy might want to be an only child."

Sloan and I looked at each other and smiled. Then we both said, simultaneously, "He takes after you. Stubborn!"

❀ Created with Vellum

www.ingramcontent.com/pod-product-compliance
Ingram Content Group UK Ltd.
Pitfield, Milton Keynes, MK11 3LW, UK
UKHW021332150625
6403UKWH00025B/213